Books by Tom Bailey

On Writing Short Stories *(2000)*

A Short Story Writer's Companion *(2001)*

The Grace That Keeps This World
(forthcoming in 2004 from Etruscan Press)

Crow Man

CROW MAN

Stories by
TOM BAILEY

etruscan press

ETRUSCAN PRESS
P.O. BOX 9685
SILVER SPRING, MD 20916-9685

WWW.ETRUSCANPRESS.ORG

1 2 3 4 5 6 7 8 9 0

PUBLISHER'S CATALOGING-IN-PUBLICATION
BAILEY, TOM, 1961-
    CROW MAN : STORIES / BY TOM BAILEY.
    P. CM.
    ISBN 0-9718-228-8-3

    1. SOUTHERN STATES--FICTION.   I. TITLE.

PS3602.A555C76 2003   813'.6
                           QBI03-700585

Acknowledgments

I am grateful to the following publications in which these stories originally appeared, some in slightly different form: *DoubleTake:* "Snow Dreams," *High Plains Literary Review:* "Detroit," *Antietam Review:* "The Cutting," The Artful Dodge: "Here," *Puerto del Sol:* "Prison," *New Myths/MSS:* "Clearing," Other Voices: "The Archaeological Society of Dancing Rabbit Creek," *Southern Exposure Magazine:* "The Well," *The Crescent Review:* "McCommas," *The Greensboro Review:* "Crow Man."

I am grateful as well to *The Pushcart Prize 2000 XXIV* for reprinting "Snow Dreams" and to *New Stories from the South and Streetsongs: New Voices in Fiction* for reprinting "Crow Man."

I would also like to thank the National Endowment for the Arts, whose generous and timely support helped immeasurably in the writing of this collection of stories, and I would like to express my appreciation to the Eastern Frontier Society, which awards residencies on Norton Island in Maine, for their deep commitment to writers and artists.

For my mother, Elizabeth,

and my father, Captain C. T. Bailey, USMC

Contents

Crow Man

Snow Dreams

I

The side door cracks open. I expect my eldest—dark, curly-headed Gary David—but it's my eighteen-year-old, blond Kevin, who slides in from outside, red-eyed and sheepish. I look him up and down as I hold the bowl and beat the batter. He's standing, hands pocketed, casting around the kitchen, glancing at the sink, the clock, the floor, the beamed ceiling, the smoking Upland. I've tried to raise my boys like I've managed to train every dog I've ever owned—with a biscuit in my left hand and a switch in my right—and I'm burning now to smack this son of mine with the accusation of what he knows is right, because I brought up both of them to know better than to drink and ever handle a gun. I wait for Kevin's eyes to finally meet mine and then, using a firm gaze, I give him a spank-hard look. He glances away, ashamed, I think, and I go back to pouring out our pancakes, reach for the boiling coffee.

There's a low scuff-kick at the door, and Kevin has to unstick his hands from his Carhartts to open it for Gary David, loaded up past his chin with split wood. To see my two grown sons standing side by side, I imagine folks could get the idea my Susan's made a practice of visiting long, lazy afternoons with the postman—summer day to winter night different as these two boys are. Kevin's more simply the spitting image of who I used to be before I suddenly, at the age of nineteen, while serving my time in 'Nam, split out of my issue with a last thirty-seven-pound three-and-a-quarter-inch growing spurt, before I rolled over forty-five and my own bright-blue eyes dimmed, and I got fixed with these squareish, silver-rimmed bifocals, when I still had all of my own straw-blond, thick, and wavy hair. Standing next to him, Gary David—both in looks and in his shyness and care—mirrors his granddaddy, Susan's black-headed, part-Onondaga daddy, as if he'd sat up in the grave and lurched back out into the world for one more tall, stiff try at things.

Another, bigger difference between them is that my youngest, Kevin, is the first of us Hazens to go on to school past the twelfth grade, taking classes now down at the local junior college in Canton. Next year, though, he wants to transfer full-time to Cortland State. He wants to live over three hours away and have us pay for him to earn himself a real degree. The first two times he mentioned this I felt the pressured dollar sign of it ticking bomb-big behind my left eye. The third time I exploded, yelling out before Susan could grab my knee and squeeze, *You just want to be on the parental dole your whole goddamn life!* You don't want to have to ever work for a living! Gary David, who's more sensible about these things, is going to be a carpenter after me. He'll find himself a nice girl like that Anne Burke whose family's lived outside Sebattis near long as we Hazens have. He'll marry and name his first boy Gary. But what I find most curious in their natures is that while Gary David was born with the heart and desire, born with the *belief* in the building, his brother Kevin has the better hands, a sharper eye for the truths of wood grains and the absolute honesty of plumb lines. Though perhaps even more strange still is that these two boys—these two men—aged a good five years apart and night-and-day opposite as they are, can be such good friends.

Gary David's sniffing strong over Kevin. "You leave any at the brewery?" he asks. "Who was it over, not that Jeanie Prescott again?" By not answering, Kevin convicts himself. "Aw, Kev . . . ," Gary David starts and gently sets down the wood like you wouldn't expect a boy to—even while he's talking to Kevin—being considerate of his mother sleeping upstairs. Kevin simply stands with his hands in his pockets, blinking, red-eyed. He's brought this girl around once or twice, and I guess she's green-eyed cute enough for dating. But she's from *New York City* of all places, just going to school up here in our North Country so she can ski seven months of the year, and she's not one of us or even remotely of our kind.

Two weeks ago Kevin asked me if he could skip his buck this season, and when I asked and eyed him why, he confessed it was because this Jeanie didn't *like* it. She didn't want him to go because she didn't think hunting was *right*. "No," I said to him, "no, you can't *skip* it," and stood up and left him standing there, more abrupt with him than I'd meant to be I guess, but too full of the voice-shaking responsibility of it right then to speak reasonably. This responsibility which was my father's responsibility before mine and his father's responsibility before him: the necessity of fulfilling our tags toward stocking three freezers to get us through one of these no-fooling winters again. If we want to eat, that is.

For us, deer season's not a matter of plaqueing a staring head nor congratulating ourselves over a rack of horns. For us, hunting's as crucial as surrounding every inch of spare space under our extra-wide porch and eaves with carefully cut, dried, and split wood—never imagining, not even able to imagine nor capable of comprehending in the blistering chainsaw heat of summer that we could ever in twelve straight hard winters use all we've stacked, and then and again stumped equally as incredulous every May when we have to scramble up the last skinny sticks and shavings of bark to heat the freezing kitchen at 5:00 A.M. This one single and unforgiving truth, out of which the responsibility I'm speaking was born: that it's already time to start the dragging and sawing and splitting again that very same afternoon if we're going to be ready for the first freeze come September. It's all about living up here—*surviving*—and so far as I'm concerned there *is* no difference between the two, but it's the huge *difference* between us Hazens and a lot of other folk who don't know or have any idea at all about the cold.

I cut my eyes at the clock. It's already three minutes past our 2:30 A.M. time to have left and be gone. I get up with my plate, rinse it off in the sink. My boys follow behind me doing the same, and then we grab our gear, ease out the door, and crunch across the crust of snow to the truck.

It's a thirty-minute drive in to our spot, winding back through the preserve and up and across Big Cloud Mountain onto a half-oval of road bordered to the east by an icy brook. Having wound and humped to be here by three, we sit silently in the truck and stare through the glare of our head-lights. A teal-colored Chevy and a brown Impala squat parked in our space. A neon-pink bumper sticker on the truck shouts: THIS BUCK HUNTS! We pop the doors and climb out into the shadow dark, and it doesn't take a flashlight to show us by the heavy frosted glass that these fellows must've come in last night, before gun season started.

I'm quick to anger, but only a few things make me mad. If these men have broken one rule to get their deer, they won't hesitate to break another or another after that. They're the kind of men who, I know, *will do what it takes*. I knew their kind in 'Nam, and I could tell some stories of things they're capable of that would make your hair go straight. I've known their kind here at home, too, watched them do carpentry, say, on a government job like HUD. You'd tear out that already straightened hair to see the work these men do, screwing everyone but themselves. When I have nightmares of evil in this world, it always comes to me in this man-shape of sloppiness and a too-easy, unearned return. And it's this evil that I'm constantly on guard against—my mission I guess—what in the passing on of an honest way of living this life I hope to give the strength of to my two sons, a strength which they'll have to call upon to fight against it long after I'm gone.

Gary David breaks off the cold snap of silence. "What do you think, Dad?"

I try to put the best face on it I can. I tell myself: *There're twenty thousand acres in front of us.* We'll turn our backs on their tracks and head the other way.

"Get the rifles, Gary David," I say.

The moon's up, spotlight bright. I lead and Gary David and Kevin follow. We walk down a gentle slope and then we begin the climb. The hill goes steep, mountains suddenly steeper. With all the clothes and the silly shell bag I've got slung over my shoulder, I feel heavy and robotic, old. Gary David and Kevin pitched in and bought the bag for me last

Christmas, and though to me it seems worse than useless with rifles on a one-day hunt, the least I can do to avoid the waste is to put it to work and carry it for them. It's unscuffed, though off-colored by dust, too stiff and strangely new and—for comfort anyway—a little too close to the size and shape of a woman's purse. My own .30-.06 shells I still keep safe in looped elastic over my breast pocket the way my father did, the same way my grandfather carried his. My boys stay right behind me the whole while, young, walking easily, their puffed breath lightly silvering.

Shots ring out into the moonlight at 3:53 A.M. They slap, *bang bang bang bang bang bang*, and then echo, booming between the rows of hills. Then there're two guns, three. The first one's reloaded and starts in again, *bang bang bang bang bang bang*. All of them rage away. There are a few distinct cracks. A pop. Then there's silence, a harder and stiller silence now, it seems, for having been disturbed so violently. Waiting crouched in the aftermath of the ambush, my body's tensed tight, reminded of war. It's against the law to shoot until first light, but from our right, from the east, we hear a thin but distinct, "Ya-*hooooo!*" Weekend blasters, sons-of-a-goddamn-bitches, crazy men. We angle even more sharply southwest away from them, push on, marching faster, in deeper, and then on faster and farther and in deeper still.

On the downside of a saddle-humped mountain, in a circled clearing, we stop for a coffee break, eat the sugared pancakes we pocketed along, the close winter sky graining a gray hint of light. Sitting in the dark, under a brightening sky, the cold surrounding us hard and crisp and clear as a shield, warm deep down inside our Carhartts, I think how it's times like these, moments like this pure still moment, that make me glad of who I am and that I've got two sons to remind me of it, to line the path and keep me on it, sons who'll carry on this life and the respect for it long after I'm gone. And it's in this simple flash of living that I can see the war and the killing I did clearly, the good it did for me, perhaps the only good it did for any of us: it helped me to recognize moments like this one, to note and appreciate them in a way and feel them with a white-flared intensity I would never've known if I hadn't ever cared and feared so for life, and not just my own.

I take a sip of the hot coffee and glance at my sons. In this sudden second I nearly manage to tell them I love them— both of them—different as they are and always will be for me, and that I'm glad they're here with me now, but even thinking to blurt out *I love you* shrinks my throat tight to strangling. I think, *This is what it means to be out here more than anything, deeper even than the professed and hammered-home responsibility*. And I suddenly realize the obvious untold reason I snapped at Kevin for not wanting to come hunting with us this season. The truth I know deep down's I couldn't live without either one of them. I cast back the dregs of my coffee and snuff my sleeve, manage to croak a harsh, "We'll never get a goddamn deer if you girls keep lollygagging." They shuffle to their feet, and then we start again on our mission march.

The country we now find ourselves in has changed from fat oak and maple. Now it's rock-rugged, spruce-filled, and shale-scaled. A tremendous valley opens out to our left, and in the speck bottom of it there's an iced-blue mountain lake sparkling silver with the first rayed flashings of sunshine. We'll never hound down a buck like this and, ready or not, it's time for me to plan a strategy and split us up. I pick the first suitable tree for Kevin, a curiously forked spruce with a wide view of this expanse, the natural path ridgeline coming up and the new day. We leave him there, looking sleepy-headed, but safe in the knowledge that the hard march has sweated the last of the alcohol out of him, and then Gary David and I push on and up and over the long slope. I place him at the top of the next piney ridge. Then I push on up and down and around along the same ridge for another half mile.

The single beech I find has a great sky-reaching spread of limbs, and I squirm out a comfortable way to wedge myself in, sweeping the open V-sights of my Remington .30-.06 over the maze of thickets and snow below. It's winter's dawn and we're ready and waiting, the opening daylit hour of the first day of hunting season each year when the most bucks are shot, before they've been alerted to the fact they're in season again, and we're far enough out in these woods that I don't think we'll have any trouble with idiots and their carelessness. I think how I would've driven myself and my boys another five miles simply to escape them and the threat of some stupid accident.

Then I hear the shaking of the brush, a racked buck stumbling toward me through the thick-tangling scrub. *Impossible*, I think, but know, too, from all the stories I've ever heard or even told, the statistics I can quote, that it's exactly this unexpected moment which I should expect and for which I should be ever vigilant. I finger a cartridge out from the elastic above my chest pocket, feed it in and gently lock home the bolt, flick off my safety and snug my cheek, seat the sights, pointing the aimed V upwind. The buck's sixty yards off. He stops and sneeze-snorts a warning, and I feel the hollow hurry in my chest, the fevered, hot-to-cold itching sweat that he's somehow caught my scent or simply *sensed* me in this tree, but then he starts crashing and crunching carelessly forward toward me again—the new morning's icy light catching the flash of his huge brushlike rack.

There's an impact thump like kicking a plump pumpkin, the shot echoing crisply, and then a rush as the buck tumbles bagged heavy into a white-staticed silence. And I'm breathing hard, raspily recovering from a full dose of buck fever as I shimmy fast down the beech. My rifle seared empty, the bolt thrown open, I jump from five feet up, climb to my feet, dust the snow quickly off, and then I chamber another round.

The buck's fallen just behind a tall drift, inside a mess of thickets. Just last year my sons and I sat around the kitchen table shaking our heads over the unbelievable newspaper story of an experienced hunter who'd been gored nearly to death by a big buck he'd wounded crazy, how he'd had to crawl himself out of the woods holding onto his own spilled entrails. From where I am I can see the flecked red shining brilliantly. There's a flailed path back where he sprinted then fell.

I tiptoe in, safety off again, finger on the trigger, use the barrel to press aside the buck-colored brush, and peek carefully in.

II

The first shot slapped Kevin straight up out of an uneasy sleep where he'd been dreaming Jeanie had him pinched by the nose and was fussing and fussing at him like a crow. He staggered, grabbed the branch in front of his face, feeling the uncomfortable ache of having wedged himself by the crotch into the crotch of the odd, hairy tree, and touched the cold hurt of his exposed nose, ran the drip of it onto his sleeve.

He heard Jeanie's cawing again and then he looked straight up to see the crow alone on the top branch, laughing at him. He pointed his levered .30-.30 up at it and watched it flap slowly up and wheel away within easy reach of his sights. Rings of sound continued to bind then ripple by him, smoothing out and out until the snow cushioned the woods silent and peaceful again. Kevin wondered who had taken the shot, his father or Gary David? If either of them had taken a shot, he knew neither had missed. He himself hadn't even bothered to load his rifle. Then he heard a second flat slap. It shocked sharply past, the echoed ripples touching lightly by him again. *Good,* he thought, *because if they get two we can leave. We'd have to leave,* he thought, *or we wouldn't be able to carry out all the meat.* Though if he knew his father, *Mr. Gary Hazen,* they *would* carry out every single slab and scrap of venison and useable hoof and horn, regardless if they *could* carry it out or not. His father made a special carpenter's glue from the hooves, rigged gun-racks with the wired forelegs. He even took the incredible time necessary to hand-buff indestructible knife handles from the horns. So Kevin sat cramped and cold in the tree, hoping they had gotten two, but hoping just as hard they wouldn't get three.

The thing was, leaving Jeanie's dorm room the night before, he had promised—in fact he had *sworn* to her—that he would tell his father that morning. He had just found out himself that Friday night, but he had promised he would have it out *before* they went hunting. But, of course, he hadn't. He *had* meant to. On the way home he had stopped in at the Lantern and had eight beers to pump himself up for it and, sitting at the bar glowing gold, he had felt cocksure, strong, thinking how maybe he'd just kick his goddamn father's ass, tell him to fuck the hell off and mind his own business—and not just about this either, but about transferring down to State when Jeanie did to earn a four-year degree, about hunting, cutting and splitting all that ridiculous firewood year in and year out, about becoming a carpenter, the whole bullshit dump-truck-load full of it—but when he'd climbed out of his beaten Dodge in front of the house at 2:00 A.M., he'd felt the cold. He'd felt suddenly too tired to hash or duke it out. Somehow he'd scratched at the door and had stepped into the warm kitchen without saying anything. Then they were in the truck and then, head down, paying for the beers and no sleep with every uphill step, he'd hiked way the hell out here, and now he was in this tree and now he was hoping his father and his brother both had gotten their precious bucks so he could go the hell home and get some sleep.

Kevin glanced at his watch. Nearly two and a half hours had passed since his father and brother had left him. The morning sunshine flashed, glittering gold.It was amazingly cold for that time of year, but after three winters of hardly any snow or any serious North Country cold, the old men at the diner had predicted last week's November blizzard far back in the strangest wet, chilly August any of them had ever seen or even heard tell about. Kevin himself had to admit he liked the snow. There was something blanket-comfortable about it. And in the snow he didn't mind the cold so much. Jeanie was from the City, from Queens actually, and she didn't like the cold. She did like to ski, though, and so the snow had grown up as a bond between them.

Snow.

Kevin closed his eyes against the four-walled whiteness, but felt her setting up on an elbow again, watching him for his reaction. She was touching up a single hair on his chest, slowly curling it around her perfect red fingernail, queuing up the question mark of it. He'd wondered then if she wanted him to yell at her or just scream or maybe whoop for some sort of joy. But the news had knocked him out. TKOed, his dream-self stood up out of his floored body and walked out the door and down the hall and down and around the steps, out onto the perfect snow-covered campus lawn.

Then, as if he were a kid again, he was angeled out in the snow, on his back waving his arms—his wings—his legs, the sweep of his robe, and the snow was falling softly down, down and down, blanketing him, his whole body down to his tingling toes, his chest icing ice-solid, blueing his lips, sticking white to his eyelashes, softly white, padding white, and the growing weight of it white-pressing his eyelids past zigzagging reds into a deep, dark-sliding blackness: avalanched alive. That's when he'd opened his eyes to find Jeanie still staring down at him. In this snow dream his planned life died, school and a degree froze and then melted that easily away and he saw himself getting up out of the bed of some house which his smiling father and his happy goddamned brother would help him build, getting up every single morning at 5 A.M. to go work off the loan he was meeting every month on some new, stupid, shiny-red, big-tired truck, working every available odd overtime job just as his father had always done, frugal with every spare second of his whole life, just to keep the baby (then babies) in diapers, in bonnets, in pureed pears. He saw a gray lunch-boxed lunch, his own coffee thermos (bought on sale), then back to sawdust in his boots, the always-aching shoulders, earning his father's calluses, wearing his father's chosen life as if it were his own.

Then, though, he'd felt Jeanie's lips burn straight down to kiss his naked chest, reawakening him, his desire rising through the cold to hard-aching reality again. He'd rolled up from underneath it all slowly then, and their lips had met, and he'd tasted her tears, arched up to her as she gripped him, and they'd made love again and then again before he went to face him, his promise, their bond, sealing it, sealed: their future lives.

"Just goddamnit," Kevin said to himself. He scraped away from the tree and peeled back his sleeve to check his watch.

It had been nearly three hours now since they'd split up. There hadn't been any more shots, but neither had his father sent Gary David back to fetch him so that he could help them clean and strip the carcasses. He glanced around his assigned clearing. His eyes stung, felt sandpapered bald from lack of sleep. He circled them wet and then, the unloaded rifle slung over his shoulder, he worked himself loose from his set stand, and started down the tree. He'd use the shots as an excuse to go see.

The two sets of boots tracked an easy path through the snow, his father's footsteps bigger, pressed deeper, and then Gary David's smaller and lighter, pressed just inside the trail breaking bigger tracks, his older brother trying unsuccessfully—or so it seemed to Kevin, it had always seemed this way to Kevin—to fill them. And as he trudged on after them, purposefully stepping just off their beaten path, making himself do the harder work of breaking new snow, he couldn't help but think to himself that as much as he loved his big brother, when it came to their father he also thought of him as a bit of a strung puppet, a dummy for the things their father wanted him to think and say.

Inside a stand of wind-strafed pine, Kevin stopped where he could see his father had set Gary David to give him a view of the entire valley. He saw where the tracks stopped to go up, but Gary David wasn't there. He circled the tree. On the other side, his father's bigger boots trudged off, and then he saw where Gary David had jumped down into them, sinking into his tracks again. Kevin's first panged thought was that his father had come back for his brother but not for him. Then he noticed both sets of tracks headed out. Neither set pointed back. And then standing under the pine puzzling down, Kevin grinned, and then standing alone under the tree in the snow patting over his pockets to confirm it, he laughed out loud: his *father* had been carrying the shell bag!

In their marched hurry, and because it was not the way the Hazens had *always done things*—not the way *his father's father* had done it and *his father's father's father* before him—not a fixture, in the way his dad had orchestrated, ordered, and directed every hunt for the past eight years that Gary David and he had been traipsing through these woods after him—he'd simply and ridiculously forgotten to dole out their ammo to them.

But Kevin saw his own caught dilemma: it was as obvious as it could be that for the past three hours he hadn't even tried to load his rifle. He'd been sitting in his stand, sound asleep, dreaming. *Unforgiveable.* And his father wouldn't forgive or let him forget about it either—not ever. Kevin could hear the told story of it over and over again during their clinking breakfasts at the diner, the head-shaking and chuckles it would always get.

Gary David must have realized the mistake as soon as he'd gotten himself good and safely situated and, of course, it had been his older brother who had climbed all the way back down and who had fallen in behind their father and who was probably trudging back towards Kevin right now, sacrificing his own precious hunting time for his younger brother who hadn't even tried to load his rifle and who didn't even give a damn. Kevin felt pretty shitty about that. But he still couldn't help but smile—no matter what the consequences. The whole forgetful episode reminded him of a mistake he himself might easily have made any hour of any day of any week, but it delighted him to no end that his father had done such a typical, stupid thing. He *is* human, Kevin thought, pleased and amazed. It was a good feeling, and he stored the warmth of it away, thinking how he might very well need it sometime later that day.

He started off after them, feeling almost happy, feeling better, at least, than he had felt all day. He followed the two sets of tracks for a long while, uphill and through the snow. The first thing Kevin caught sight of was a caution road-sign flag of safety orange. He stopped, seeing, but in the harsh glare unable to imagine or make out at all what it was exactly he saw. It looked to him as if he'd caught his father scraping and groveling. He was on his knees, bowing low, inchwormed up as if he were praying in the snow, from behind the brand-new shell bag strapped on his back. Then, from ten yards, Kevin saw his brother Gary David sprawled flat, the snow red-mapped telltale around him. He heard his own howl. Shocked still, he saw the rifle barrel choked off in his father's mouth.

III

It was late afternoon: twelve hours since they'd stepped out of the truck in the clearing beside the frozen stream at 3 A.M. The temperature had risen in the earlier, full, clear sunshine, but now, with the long winter's night around them, the cold was closing in. Kevin stoked the fire, and the flames jumped wild, hissing. His father lay close beside the fire, covered as warmly as Kevin could imagine to make him. When Kevin had first recognized what had happened, he'd felt his world physically tilt, heave, then slither from beneath his feet. He'd landed, clutching snow, felt his stomach lurch and roll—he couldn't help this and it wouldn't stop—then, still stringing spit, he'd crawled quickly forward toward them, patting blindly over the crushed and blinding snow. Kevin had let go of his brother's pipe-cold arm and had reached out and touched his father's wrist to feel a thin pulse hiding just below the skin. With the realization that his father was still alive, he'd forced himself to shove his brother's death aside and had pulled himself up through the horror of it with one single-minded, numbed-stupid, but saving thought: *fire.*

After he had kindled the wet sticks and built the licking flames hot enough to support the frozen limbs and had scavenged and carried back armload after armload of wood from beneath snow drifts to keep the flames going strong, Kevin had taken the careful time necessary to wrap his father's sticky head, torn cheek and blown jaw in his own T-shirt before realizing he, too, was starting to chill, to chatter dangerously himself.

Of course, Kevin had no idea just how seriously cold it would get that night. If his father had ever allowed them to pack along a radio, he would have heard the flurried broadcast of warnings, and if he had, he might have pushed on through the dark toward the heater in the truck without waiting for his mother to get worried enough to send the Rangers out after them, knowing that if there was no chance of making it there was also very little choice but to try. The coming cold, sweeping into the snow left by the blizzard in the mountains that night was expected to break every record for November, but then the actual temperature of 17 below would exceed even those record-breaking expectations. What Kevin could sense, though, even without a weather advisory on the radio, was the increasingly still and silent razor edge of the air. Even the fire seemed to be having more and more trouble breathing, the flames going thickish and slow, glowing blue, low and close over the orange-red coals. Kevin looked to his father then, but his father's eyes were rolling uncontrolled between snapping suddenly open to out-cold closed. Kevin felt a sudden futile flaring. No matter what happened to them then, he wanted his father to know that what had happened to Gary David that morning hadn't been his fault. It had obviously been an *accident,* and accidents happened no matter how carefully you planned or dreamed or wished for something else. *Didn't he know something about that?* He wished then he had told his father that he was going to marry Jeanie, about the baby they were going to have. He'd planned to stand up and say to him: *I will live my own life, make decisions as my own man, but I will respect you and the way you raised me always.* And that's when he heard himself say out loud: "I love you, too, Dad." Kevin felt rushed through blue space. He trailed his father back to find himself seated beside him before the fire again, overwhelmed by the aftershot, shocked understanding of what, all along, his father had really been trying to teach Gary David and him about surviving in the cold. Then, without his having to think further about it or even plan, Kevin angeled his stored warmth down over his father. He closed his eyes and dreamt the Rangers stumbled upon them just before dawn.

Detroit

"Yes sir, Mr. Bubba. Dee-*troit!*" Charles Brim patted his front shirt pocket, fingered out a wrinkled pack of Kools, and circled them open. "*Dee*-troit's all I'm saying."

Bubba was sitting beside Charles Brim on an old tractor tire under the shed at the shop, hands flat on his stubby knees, staring down at the dust coating his black patent-leather boots, and listening to the young man. He pulled a blue bandana out of his back pocket and spat on it, leaned over his belly to shine his right toe, looked up from his own round face growing tall and pea-small in the black-mirrored gleam, and said, "You dreaming, son."

Charles Brim stopped fishing after the stub of cigarette. He looked at Bubba and then he shook his head. "Uh um, Mr. Bubba. No *sir*. I been working up a stash. I'm saying, if I had the cash I'd head out tonight. Hell, I'm ready to go right now. Gots everything on me that I ever own." He spread his arms wide—a tattered khaki shirt and baggy paint-spattered work pants, a doo-rag bubbled snug over his rowed hair. He dropped his arms, wagging his head, said, "Man, I'm going to get up that dough and blow—"

"You *blowing* now," Bubba said and stood up, turned his back on the young man, cutting him off. He glanced through the sun-winking diamond-shaped chain-links of the fence, out over the smokey cotton, out over the blue and red and yellow rag-bright boy and girl and woman and old man swatches of Ally's slow crew chopping its way through a jungle of tall-tufted Johnson grass—the sun edged like a razor above them. Ally's bus sat parked on the turnrow, big Ally set up on his director's chair under the shade of a blue-and-white beach umbrella, sipping something cool, some sweet young thing—looked like that Eveline Turner doing what everybody knew the word was she was up to trying to pay her own way out to Chicago—favored to fanning behind him. Bubba turned back to Charles Brim, shaking his head at these young people and vaguely coming to the remembrance of something—and then it dawned on him—the day Charles's daddy had stroked dead out there on that very crew, chopping under this same murdering sun. And thinking how, most likely, for all his talk, Charles Brim'd follow right along in his father's footsteps to the same shallow grave under the scrub pines in the Welfare Cemetery. Bubba sucked his tongue. "Um," he said to himself, feeling how horrible that was, then thumbed back over his shoulder at the choppers chopping behind them. "I hears exactly where you headed, son."

"Uh, um. No, uh." Charles Brim hadn't stopped shaking his head. "No, *sir*," he said. "That ain't right. I'm saying, I'd head out tonight. It don't matter what you says or what I gots to do neither. I'd steal from my mama's purse. I'll risk a liquor store if I gots to. I'll work like I'm slaving now—

33

eighty hours a week and no sleep. Cause I'm going to Dee-*troit*, man! I ain't drinking. I ain't even buying smokes no more until I get up North and get me one of them high-paying fact'ry jobs. I pick my butts up off'n the street and saves them's how bad I'm going to Dee-troit, Mr. Bubba!"

Bubba clucked his tongue. "Um," he said, "I bet you is the kind of no-good son would steal from his own old widowed mama too." He shook his head, pursed his lips and said, "Now you through bragging about your stub cigarettes? Now you ready to sit there quiet and listen to someone what has heard the word and learned the lesson?" Bubba looked down at Charles Brim, who was sitting with his elbows on his knees, wrists dangling the pack of cigarettes, staring between his feet, his worn-soled brown boots, his left big toe poking out, no laces, and the tongue lolling in the dust. Bubba hitched his suspenders over his belly. "All right," he said and nodded at the young man's respectful silence. "Now, didn't I have the dream too and didn't I go off to Dee-troit as a young man? And didn't I come on back here home again like everybody in this whole town know about it?"

"A rich man!" Charles Brim said and shot up ramrod-straight, grinning. He nodded his head. "I hears down at the café that's how you staked that place out to the Prim. The stash you bought your first hog with. I hears all the time how you and Mr. Ally went off partners to Dee-troit and made it big and come back here to live like kings. How now you just work here for Mr. Jack when it pleases you and ain't got nothing better to do. You on the school board! You a deacon in the church! Every colored around town call you 'Sir!' and 'Mr.!' And that's exactly what I'm talking about, man!" Charles pinched a pink-kissed butt up tight and lit it close. He took a big toke, tossed his head back and blew smoke. "DEE-*troit!*" he said.

Bubba just stared at him. Then he gathered himself and started in again. "Now you listen here, son! I am trying to tell you I done done it. I—"

But Charles wasn't listening to him. He picked up his hands and plugged his fingers in his ears so he couldn't hear. Then he started to hum loud "That Road to Glory."

I'm going to go on up that road to Glory.
Up that road!
Up that steep road
To where Gabriel blow his horn.

Bubba stood, stopped cold again, thrown off by this new tactic. Then he felt his face rush angry. "Now you listen here, son. I am trying to save—"

"Stand back, old man!" Charles Brim slapped out, shaking his head and turning his eyes down into the dust: "You the evil toad! You like the devil in my ear, old man, squatting your doubt and deception. I know the path I gots to go. I know that road! You just wants all the glory and all them riches for yourself, I know!"

"No!" Bubba said. He pointed his finger at Charles Brim, shaking. "That ain't so, son! I'm just trying to warn you. I'm trying to tell you like it really is!"

A horn blared and Bubba jumped. Then he regained himself and whirled to face it. Ally had gotten out of his director's chair and was now in the bus barreling toward them. He boo-booped the horn again, waving with one hand inside a cloud of dust. He bumped across the skinny strip of asphalt and squeezed through the gate, rolled up and then jumped off the clutch, letting the motor shudder and yank off. The bus was battered, the engine poking through the rust-eaten hood. The sides were paint-spangled red, white, and blue—BOY SCOUTS OF AMERICA lettered neatly on the panel, Xed out with black spray paint, and under that, BLOOD OF THE LAMB BAPTIST CHURCH, Xed out with black spray paint too, and under that in big green hand-brushed letters, ALLY'S CHOPPING, and painted beside it a long logo cornstalk-looking weed of Johnson grass, a brown-globbed hoe, and the red streak of a scythe. The accordion doors wheezed open, and Ally stepped down into the gravel and dust of the shop yard, lugging a big orange Igloo cooler behind him.

"Well," he smiled, rows of gold teeth gleaming all the way back in his head. "If it ain't the in-*ES*-timable *Mister* Bubba!"

Ally was a real giant—six foot four, hunched back and thick, with great long arms. His head was shaved bald, sporting a straw safari hat against the sun, and in the furnace heat his skin shone blue-black and mirror shiny as the patent-leather boots Bubba wore. He laid out his right palm for Bubba to slap, but Bubba simply nodded back, keeping his own hands pocketed.

"Ally," he said.

Ally looked down at his empty palm—shook it off with a laugh and let it drop. "All right," he said. "*Fine*. But you can't begrudge me filling up my water jug at the faucet here, *Mister* Bubba. We working Mr. Jack's land, and my niggers're dropping like. . . ." Ally stopped—for the first time noticing Charles Brim on the tractor tire under the shed—rocking back and forth and humming and singing loud with his fingers poked in his ears.

Up that road!
On up that road!
Going up that road to glory
To where the angel Gabriel blow his horn.

Ally nodded across the yard at him. "What's up with that boy?" he said.

At first Bubba wouldn't answer him. He watched Charles Brim humming and nodding under the shed with his fingers plugged up in his ears—then he sighed and said, "He *says* he's going to Dee-troit. *Says* he'd rob his own widowed mama to get there."

Ally smiled. "That right?" he said. "Hey, boy! Boy!" he yelled at him.

Charles Brim stopped his rocking. He looked around at them and then he unplugged his ears. "Afternoon, Mr. Ally."

"I hear you going to Detroit, boy."

"Yes, sir, Mr. Ally," Charles said, nodding. "I surely am. Just like that once-upon-a-time you and Mr. Bubba went off partners there."

Ally nudged Bubba. "How you plan to get there, boy? You going to fly the TWA or take the Greyhound?"

Charles Brim frowned. His eyebrows scrunched down. "Walk if I have to."

Ally broke up at that. "*Walk* to Dee-*troit!*" He hooted and slapped his knee. "Well now I can go ahead and die I guess. Now I have heard every kind of thing there is to hear. Shit, son," he said. "Do you have any idea at all where on this gigantic earth Dee-troit is?"

Charles Brim nodded, pointed straight up. "North," he said and then he picked up his hands and stuck his fingers back in his ears.

"Um!" Ally said, nudging Bubba again. "You got you a live one there," he said and circled his ear three times. "I'd stay away from that crazy field nigger if I were you, Mister Bubba. That one young field hand there's baked too long under this sun. That nigger there, *Mister* Bubba," Ally said, "is liable to go off and hurt someone." Ally laughed big at that. Then, still laughing and shaking his head, he stepped over to the faucet, set the cooler down, and reached for the handle.

Bubba watched after Ally and then he glanced back at Charles. He thought down—the black-pooled reflection of his own round-cheeked face thinking back up at him— shook his head and broke away again, glimpsed, through the glittering fence, the broken wave of choppers dried up on the turnrow beyond, waiting for water before they returned to the fire of the fields again.

"Course," Ally said, standing by the spattering faucet, one hand on his hip, still grinning. "I guess we was a little *mad* when we run off to Dee-troit ourselves."

"But we come back *home* again," Bubba said. "It's like I been trying to tell him. . . ."

"*Shit,*" Ally said and flashed his eyes at him. "Now you may not want to act like you never even knowed me in public, John L., but don't *you* be giving *me* none of that uppity city hall, school board, preacher bullshit."

Bubba flinched. He took his bandana out and wiped his forehead with it. "But we didn't *know,*" he said.

Ally nodded. "We sure hit that ole lucky jackpot square smack-dab on the lucky damn head if that's what you talking about—following that old gentleman that night. Dee-troit the start of everything either one of us has ever been. Got me my start with this bus. Now they ain't a drink I can't drink or a woman I can't have to sleep with if I want her bad enough."

Bubba was looking out over the fields again and when he didn't say anything, Ally went on.

"And you know I ain't never been able to figure you out right. What your deal is. Same money bought you that house out to the Prim. You a deacon in the church now. Got you a fat wife and kids. I even hears you bought you a piece of family ground up near the white 'piscopal cemetery to be buried in."

Ally laughed hard at that and shook his head, wiped a tear from his eye, and said, grinning gold at him, "Why you become a regular old hyp-o-crite!"

Bubba stood there in the dust under that bald sun and looked back at Ally's gold grinning at him. He looked at his smiling and then he reached out and shut off the faucet. "I guess that's full enough," he said, giving it to him. "Can't have you using up all of Mr. Jack's water, now can we?"

The smile dropped off Ally's face. He glared hard at Bubba and then, holding him with his red eyes, reached out and turned the faucet back on to splashing full. He held his hand on the handle, his big forearm screwed tight, and let the water run, even when the cooler was full and the water had overflowed. It wasted over the sides, pattering on the concrete and off into the dust, making instant mud. The two men stared at each other, then Ally relaxed his grip and twisted off the faucet. "Maybe if you hadn't hit that fellow so hard, *Mister* Bubba—" Ally shrugged. "But *you* did, John L. *You* that fucked up and killed him so that we had to scurry back to this hole town to hide out in." He bent over and screwed on the lid and hugged up the fat cooler. "See you at the café this evening, *partner*," he said with a wink. "Maybe I'll even buy you a beer for old times' sake." He picked up his gleaming smile again and lugged the Igloo over to the bus and up the stairs. He clanked up the engine and circled the yard. As he passed Charles Brim, he slowed down and yelled, "They'll always be a spot on my crew for you, boy! Just like your daddy!" He clanked up the engine, laughing, and pulled the door shut, drove out of the yard, booping the horn.

Charles didn't even look up—lost drawing numbers in the

39

dust with the long-levered lug wrench for the tractor tires—mumbling.

Bubba waited until Ally had bumped out of the yard and back across the line of asphalt onto his side of the field again before he walked over to where Charles Brim was sitting under the tractor shed, wondering how much he'd heard. He stood over him—$4.03, $7.13, $26.50, 34 cents. He shook his head, then kicked dust over the numbers with his shiny boot. "You ain't been listening to a thing anybody's said, have you, son?"

Charles Brim was squatting there, looking up at him, his face blank, as if kicking dust over the numbers had also erased his mind.

Bubba sighed. He shook his head and then he reached into his back pocket and pulled out his wallet. He spread it generously and peeled out two crisp one-hundred-dollar bills. He held them out to Charles Brim.

"Now, do you promise me you'll leave straight from here and never come back again? You swear on your soul that you'll go straight down to that depot and buy yourself a one way ticket to Dee-troit and not stop in and blow it all at the first beer joint?"

Charles just stared at him. Stared from him—drop-mouthed—to the money. Then his face glowed out into a huge grin.

"Mr. *Bubba!*" he said. "You is the saviour of my life! You is a Christian and a fine man!" Charles Brim reached for the money, but John L. folded it out of the air, made it disappear right in front of him. He clucked his tongue at him.

"Rob his own widowed mother, he says. Bragging about your stub cigarettes!" Bubba shook his head. "I done made up my mind. I'm going to save you from yourself, son," he said. "I'm going to save you from making the same mistake I did." He nodded and gave the young man a big smile and stuffed the money away from him, deep down in his pocket away from Charles Brim. Bubba reached out and gripped his shoulder. "You're going to come work for me, son. I'm going to make you heir to all I have become." And he stood back up, looking down at Charles Brim sitting stunned before him with the bestowal of this, his hands still held out in the air as if in supplication. Bubba nodded, grinned. "It's something ain't it, son," he said. He patted Charles on the shoulder again, then turned to look triumphantly through the gates at Ally and the scattered crew chopping under the brilliant blazing sun. As he took that step, he didn't see the long shadow leap up, scythelike, to reap down behind him— the pop of his own head echoing sharply close to far away again—leaving Charles Brim standing alone in the yard, breathing hard, the lug wrench gripped tight between his own two palms.

"Lord," Charles said, "oh, Jesus, Mr. Bubba," staring down at what he'd done. He dropped the lug wrench and then dropped to his knees in the dust—lifted the wallet, but had to roll the old body over to get at the front pockets. Charles Brim stumbled up then, already running—the sun north-pulsing a glorious golden blare of light on the steep road beyond.

The Cutting

With thanks to James Failing

Bill Buckner climbed out of his Ford truck, turned to catch his daughter down, then slammed the door. Caile raced on ahead of him to flutter the chicken coop, and he followed in his tall polished boots, tugging at his belt, tucking in his madras shirt, and smiling.

"We got the sign, Joe?"

"Sure enough, Mr. Buckner," Joe Walker said. He thumbed up at the sky—a tremendous high clean blue, not a cloud in sight.

The hog stood alone in the shack pen—the shoats hugging up against their side of the boarded fence to keep an eye on him. A sow lay plopped on her side in the mud. When the boar grunted, the soft white piglets ran away from her in stampede terror, then rushed straight back to suckle close, but still wide-eyed and wary.

Willie Pitts met Buckner's grip. "You sure you want Caile to see this, Bill?"

Buckner smiled at him. "Hell, that's why I'm here, Willie."

"Well," Willie said, nodding, and they stood together looking at the big hog in the pen.

There was the squawk and flutter of chickens, feathers flying. "Caile!" Buckner yelled. His daughter stopped and looked at him, biting back her bottom lip. She had blonde hair and great green eyes and she stood looking at her daddy and the other men—the men all looking back at her, the hog standing alone in the center of the pen.

Willie Pitts whistled up and down. "My, she's a pretty thing, Bill!"

"Isn't she?" Buckner smiled. He hooked his daughter in with his finger. "Come on over here, Beautiful." She walked over and he lifted her high under the arms and sat her on top of the rail.

"It stinks," she said and pinched her nose, and the other men smiled at her, and Buckner laughed big.

"My little tulip," he said. He held her by the waist and nuzzled her hair from behind.

"Gentlemens." Joe Walker pointed at the sky again. "We got the sign."

Willie looked around at them. "All right then." He gave Jamie the nod. Jamie looped the rope into a quick slipknot as Willie rang the pail. "Come on, son," Willie called to the hog. He reached over the railing and unslung the gate. Clucked his tongue. "Come on, boy," he said, dangling the oats and banging the bucket with the flat of his hand. The hog trotted straight for the oats, and Willie let him bury his thick head right up to his neck. Then he took the oats away, tempting him.

Buckner rested his forearms on the top railing. "Jesus,

Willie. That sumbitch must weigh near goddamn four hundred pounds."

Willie looked up. "Four hundred and sixty-five exactly."

"Get him cut you going to have you some sweet mellow meat," Joe Walker said.

Willie smiled. "I've been dreaming of a Christmas ham."

Jamie shook his head—standing with the rope off behind them. Called out from there, "Hog like that take a man's hand straight off."

Buckner turned all the way around and looked at him. He grinned. "Hey. Goddamn," he said, smiling. "You aren't afraid of him, are you, Jamie?"

"Shit," Jamie said. He hitched at his pants, already buckled to the boy-skinny first notch. "Shit, man. I'm just saying's all I'm saying. I'm just telling you," he said.

The big boar eyed Willie, snuffling, then tiptoed up for the oats. As he dipped toward the bucket, Jamie flung the lasso around his neck, but the hog saw it coming, snorted back, and slipped the noose, shying toward the pen, where he stood pawing up the dust, bull big.

"That fat pig quicker than he look," Jamie said, coiling in the empty line.

"That ain't no 'pig,' boy," Buckner said.

"That's a man!" Caile said and pointed at the hog and laughed gleefully.

"That's a man all right, Darlin'," Buckner said and oinked into her honied hair.

The big hog eyed the men and Caile's pitched laughing. He took two steps in—Willie clanging the pail—one step back, two more steps in, tentatively stretching out his neck, his nose pink-soft, wet and quivering.

"Now!" Willie said, and Jamie snaked the rope through the air, bit all his skinny weight against it. The boar stood with the noose around his neck, blinked twice—then he exploded, bucking. The chickens cackled across the yard. The sow scrambled up, piglets panicking back and forth between her legs.

"Whoa!" Joe yelled. Willie leapt in. Buckner left Caile safe high on the railing. The big hog dug back, dug in, grunting like a tractor diesel against the weight of the four men. "We got him now!" Buckner whooped, hauling hard. Then the hog shifted forward and bore straight down on them. Caile screamed out. Jamie dropped the rope and ran. Willie rolled out of the charge of the hog's hooves, Joe and Buckner still holding onto the line, taking quick advantage of the slack, looping the rope around the stub pole sunk into the yard. Willie added in his weight again, and together the three men worked the leverage to reel the hog in. When his head bumped the post, Jamie danced in with the rope.

"Come on!" Buckner yelled at him, his face gone brute red.

Jamie looped the line, looped it again, lashing down the hog's jaws, mounting his head firmly against the post.

"That a way! Now over! On three...."

The men shouldered in together, shoved again.

"Sonofabitch!" Buckner whooped.

The hog leaned back against them, everyone grunting, the men leaning in, and the hog held them, holding, and then he threw over in a dust of flailing hooves, thrashing sharp—the men scrambling to catch those kicked knives— and all the while the boar snorting and writhing to twist free from the pole and warning his teeth at them, squealing.

Buckner twirled the last knot. "Hog-tied!" he yelled, and threw his hands in the air.

Willie Pitts climbed slowly off the ground, dusting his palms against his jeans. "Everybody all right?"

Jamie lay scrunched in the dirt, gripping his forearm between his knees.

"Hey," Willie said. "You all right, Jamie?" He knelt in the

dust beside him. "Let me see, son." But Jamie wouldn't open up to him, lay with his forearm squeezed between his knees, and Willie had to squat him and pry his red fingers apart to see—the gore gone bone deep. Willie whistled. "Jesus," he said. Then he said, "Okay. All right. You're going to be all right, Jamie. You're going to be fine." He pulled Jamie up out of the dust and guided him to a barrel seat beside the fence. Jamie sat on the barrel, sweating, looking straight up at the sky while Willie worked on him—grabbing out a handkerchief and knotting it tight to ebb the cut.

Buckner followed Caile's eyes—her forehead knitted down. "Oh, hell," he said. He tipped her chin up and smiled. "Now don't you go on worrying about it, Honey." He tousled her blonde hair and winked, laughed. "Ain't nothing twenty or thirty stitches can't fix."

Willie stood up from the cut. "We'll get you to the hospital soon as. . . ."

"I told him," Jamie said. He looked down from the sky and at Willie and he said, "Didn't you hear me tell him?"

Willie looked at him. "I guess I heard you tell him all right."

Joe Walker stood off from them, his old black-handled lock blade out, scraping it back and forth across the concrete steps of the smokehouse. He held it up and touched it to his tongue. Spat the nick of blood. The hog lay roped in the dust, his balls pooched plump as goose eggs.

"Gentlemens."

Joe Walker knelt down behind him and weighted the hog's balls up on the flat scale of his palm. "Umm," he said. Then he gave the right one a good slap—grunting the hog out of breath—sending him crazy again, thrashing, trying to kick out his hobbled legs.

Buckner turned his head. "I can't watch this part," he said. But he peeked back through his spread fingers and smiled for his daughter—Caile watching Jamie, frowning. "Hey," he said and fingered her ribs until she smiled, laughed, twisting, and squealed, "Daddy!"

"You don't want to blink and miss this now!" he warned her.

Joe Walker waited for the hog to calm, then he took up the knife. Buckner put a finger to his lips. His boots shuffled the gravel. Joe Walker bent close and cut. The hog erupted into the sky.

He sat back on his heels away from the hog's thrash and squalorings, and yelled over, "You got to sit on him, Jamie! I don't want to hurt him no more than I got to."

"You *crazy*?" Jamie held out his cut arm. "I ain't *sitting* on him. I *told* you. Goddamned if I'm sitting on him."

Buckner glared at Jamie, then he hawked and spat the dust. He stepped up and saddled the hog's ribs. Nodded. "Go ahead, Joe."

There was blood on Joe Walker's hands. It gleamed the knife blade. The hog's eyes had milked white into his head, and his squealings ripped the air, but he was roped to the pole by the neck, his legs hobbled, Bill Buckner squatting on his chest, and there was no place for him to go as Joe Walker slit again and wriggled his fingers up and in. Joe pulled the hog's testicles out and cut the cords—dumped them into the pail of oats. He used his shirtsleeve to wipe the sweat off his face. "Hand me that salt," he said. Willie handed Joe the bag of road salt, then handed him a can of burnt oil, and Joe salted the cuts, then poured the oil on thick, kneading the black messy stuff in.

"You can get up off him now, Mr. Buckner."

Buckner climbed off, careful of the hog's hooves, but the cut hog just lay there, didn't move. Joe Walker pushed up from his knees—unhobbled the hog's legs, then raised his head to lift the noose. But even untied, the big hog didn't try to struggle up, just lay there on his side in the dust, big and white with the black oil smeared over the loose sack of skin, lay there, just breathing. It was quiet without the fight of squealing, the shoats and sows and piglets quiet too, nosed against the pen, the men standing in a silent ring around him.

Caile leaned over, getting a naked shot at the mess of the hog's balls, powdered with oats in the bucket, and Buckner leaned up close behind and smiled into his daughter's ear, "And that's all you ever got to know about men, Honey."

Caile turned to look at him. She glanced back at the hog's balls dumped in the bucket—the big hog fat on its side in the pen. Jamie sat on the barrel, holding his arm, the pigs snuffling their pink noses at him. Then she jumped from the rail and raced across the yard to fluster the chickens again.

"Caile!" Buckner stood there, hands on his hips. He could feel the other men smiling at him.

Here

1

When my dad resigned his commission in the Marines, we drove all those miles from Florida to West Virginia, where he'd taken a new job. He said he wanted to see how much money he could make as a civilian designing airplanes instead of flying them for peanuts for Uncle Sam. But this wasn't the first time we'd moved following my dad. We'd been stationed in North Carolina and Texas, in Virginia, Alabama, and Georgia. The fact of the matter was I'd never stayed in the same school for more than a year. I sat in the backseat of our old blue 1963 Oldsmobile station wagon, surrounded by our things, and watched over my mother's shoulder as my world turned from white sands to rolling red-brown to mountain green. My mother looked back over the seat at me and smiled. My dad had his black aviator sunglasses on. He stared straight ahead as he drove. The

Mayflower truck was somewhere on the road behind us. It would meet us wherever we found ourselves. It always had.

We'd moved over a weekend, and Monday afternoon my mother dropped me off at the public pool. My dad had started his new job that morning, and she didn't want me moping around the new house anymore. "You're an old hand at this, Timmy," she said, reaching across me to open my door. "Make some friends." I sat in the seat beside her staring straight ahead, and then I grabbed my towel and climbed out. "I'll be back to pick you up at four. Have *fun!*" she said, and smiled at me from behind her cat-eyed sunglasses. She left me standing on the sidewalk and drove off to finish unpacking the boxes the Mayflower men had left.

I paid my fifty cents to get in and staked out a space for myself by laying out my big beach towel by the fence. A few kids looked over at me. When you're the new kid, you get used to being stared at all the time. It was the usual public pool scene, starring mothers with their shrieking kids and high school girls sunning on towels set out whispering close, a concrete basketball court at the far end with a running game going for the older boys. The pool itself frothed with a frenzy of kids, while bored lifeguards with white junk on their noses sat above it all in their high chairs twirling their whistles. I walked over to stand at the edge of the three-foot end, hugging myself. I'd gotten used to spending my summer days at the beach, which I'd been able to walk to from our last house. The hazy, humid mountain weather left me cold.

I'd just sighted out a lane and aimed my hands over my head to dive in when this kid flailed his way in front of me, quacking like a duck. And then I noticed what else was so odd about him: he had two broken arms, the casts wrapped up in clear kitchen trash bags so they wouldn't get soaked. He was swimming with his glasses on, his eyes screwed small behind the thickness of the lenses, and he had the biggest head I'd ever seen on a boy my age, outsized as a melon. With his head attached to his scrawny body by the whipcord of his neck, he appeared before me the living proof of some sort of alien, a regular freak of nature. He looked up at me standing there caught staring down at him like that, cocked his head sideways, and spluttered, "Whatsch upch Donaldsch?" Then he shouted out a wild Woody Woodpecker laugh and flapped away, slapping up waves. The other kids swimming in front of him did their best to clear out of his way.

"Great," I said, shivering, and shook my head as I dipped my big toe in. *"Wonderful."* This freak was my first prospect for a friend.

I watched after him as he paddled across the pool to the other side. One of the older girls in a pale-blue bikini was sunning herself on the edge, and when he splashed in front of her she shot up, grabbing for her top, whirled around and sent a slap of water straight into his face. His glasses washed off, spinning him around flailing after them. They sank and he sputtered blindly away, loosed zany as a windup duck in a tub.

When he banged into my end of the pool again, the blond lifeguard was standing beside me, hands on his hips, waiting for him.

"You know the rules, Willy," he said. "Three strikes and you're out. No splashing, and I've already warned you twice."

The kid stopped, dropped his chin. Then he spun and made a break for open water. The lifeguard leapt in up to his waist, snagged him by the back of his purple trunks and dragged him backward through the water, the kid kicking and screaming for all he was worth.

He left the kid perched on the edge of the pool under his chair, hugging his skinny legs like some kind of ugly,

pouting, big-headed, broken-armed, trash-bagged gar-
goyle. None of the other kids even bothered to look at him.
I watched the whole thing. I waited for a lane and then I
dove in. Back in Florida, I'd just joined the swim team when
my dad decided it was time for us to leave. I stretched my
dive out into a long glide, sliding by the underwater churn
of legs. I made it in one breath all the way to where the kid's
glasses rested on the bottom of the pool.

I broke the surface close by the girl in the pale-blue
bikini and swam over to the lifeguard's chair and held the
kid's glasses up to him. He stared past me. "Here," I said,
waving the glasses in front of his face. "I found these over
there." He tried to focus down on me then, and I pressed the
glasses on him. Then I realized his hands were wrapped up
in the bags.

It was more than I'd bargained for. I opened the things up
and held them out for him. "Look, I found your glasses," I
said again. He bent over as if it were the most natural thing
in the world, while I held the glasses for him so he could slip
his face between the arms of the frame. I left them hanging
on his ears.

He blinked back at me through the drips of water, his
eyes screwed small again. He looked at me like that, and
then he glanced around the pool. He looked at the girl in the
pale-blue bikini. Then he checked the lifeguard. He turned
his big head back to pinpoint me with his gaze.

"William Henry Smalls the Third," he announced and
held out the bagged edge of his cast. I took the corner and
shook it. "I'm Tim," I said. "My friends back in Florida
called me Timmy." I was hanging onto the edge of the pool.

From above us, the lifeguard called down, "Hey, no talking to the prisoner."

"Screw you," William Henry Smalls the Third said up to
him under his breath. He was a little, scrawny, quirky pain-

in-the-ass kind of kid. I liked him immediately. "Willy," he said to me, "my parents call me Willy."

"Okay, Willy," I said. The lifeguard had stopped twirling his whistle and stood to haul up his trunks, staring straight-faced down at us, so I pushed off the edge and backstroked out into the middle of the pool to wait out Willy's sentence.

When he was released at the end of his fifteen minutes, Willy cannonballed into the water, trying to splash the life-guard, but only sent up a poor little sploosh.

"He'll never catch me again," he called out as he flailed his way over to me.

I nodded at his casts. "What'd you do?" I asked.

"Broke 'em," he replied. "Both of them. Compound frac-tures. Two pins in the right elbow. The left wrist may never be the same."

I wanted to know how he'd managed that, seeing as how most kids broke one arm at a time. He told me he'd fallen out of the top of a tree. "*The* tree actually. You haven't been to my house yet. But in the front yard we've got this tree, an old pine. I was nearly to the top. I mean I had it in my sights. But those limbs get thin as the air up there." He shrugged. "My dad said he wished I'd've broken my neck." Willy grinned at that. "My dad's a real sonofabitch. 'The Bastard,' I call him." Then he looked me over good. "You're not from around here, are you? Nobody around here would wear those kind of skimpy Speedo trunks to the pool. Florida, you said. So, what's your story? Tell it from the beginning and don't leave out anything. If you've got any good parts, I want to know all about it. Maybe your dad got fired or something and your family had no where else to go. But make it interesting, you see what I mean? Don't let the thing drag. Pick up the pace."

"Well," I said, "we just moved here from Florida this weekend."

Willy shook his head. He held up his right bag. "Look, don't bore me. I already know that. Come on, get on with it. Do you have a good-looking older sister, for instance? How come you came to West Virginia of all the god-forsaken places in the world to go?" He looked around. "Look at all these inbreds. I mean why *here?*"

I felt my face flush red. "You're an asshole," I said, feeling my arms knot up. I pointed my finger at his chest the way my dad did when he got mad at me. "I didn't have a choice. If it'd been up to me, I'd be anywhere else but here."

Wally threw his head back at that and shouted out his Woody Woodpecker laugh. "That's it!" he cried. "You got the hang of it now. Cut loose! Don't hold back! Get it all out!"

That afternoon by the pool I told Willy the whole story. I told him how much I'd grown to like northern Florida—enough to want to stay there—how white the sand was there, how you could swim all year. You could fish from the canals and go crabbing off bridges. I told him how we bought chicken parts and left them out in the sun to rot, how we baited our nets with the stink to catch the blue-shelled crabs. I told him about the turtles that you could ride if you caught them out on the sands. They were that big. There was an old fellow who lived next door to us there, Mr. Beardon, who painted the names we gave the turtles on their shells, PINKY and BOB. And when we caught them again, we'd find the shells had grown around the paint, curling weird twisted designs. I told him about a hurricane that had come howling through one night and ripped up our mailbox and sent it flying down the street.

"Cool," Willy said nodding as he listened to me. "Go on."

We climbed out to sit on the edge of the pool, and I told him about my best friend back in Florida, a guy named Jimmy Eddleston. His family had belonged to the circus.

54

They had a trampoline in their backyard and rings you could swing from, a net to catch you if you fell. I told him about my other friends there, too, Doug McGill and Peter Tyler. We'd been good buddies, but now I'd probably never see them again. I never saw any of my friends again once we pulled up stakes and left a place. I told him the truth about being an only child, which was that it sucked.

And I was starting to elaborate about other things—like that the real reason my dad had resigned his commission in the Corps, I suspected, wasn't the money at all but because he'd been passed over a third time for a promotion to Major—when I heard my mother call my name, "Tim!" She was leaning against the outside the fence. It was already 4:00.

"That's your *mom?*" Willy said, his eyes swirling up behind his glasses. He whistled. "Who needs an older sister!"

I helped him up, hauling him under the arms, and then grabbed my towel on the way to introduce him. My mother had her blonde hair pinned up in a bun and she was wearing a sleeveless, white, button-down shirt and jean shorts, sandals like everyone in Florida wore. She shifted her green eyes from me to Willy and back to me as we walked up. She raised her eyebrows.

"Mom," I said, "this is my new friend, Willy."

Willy stood right against the fence, ogling up at her. He stepped back to give her a bow. "William Henry Smalls the Third at your service, ma'am."

My mom looked at me. Then she laughed. "It's a pleasure to meet you, Mr. Smalls."

"The pleasure," Willy said, turning to wink at me, "is all mine, ma'am."

As Mom and I walked together out into the parking lot where our station wagon was idling at the curb, Willy called after me through the fence, "See you tomorrow, Timmy!" My mother waited until we were in the car before she asked,

"What happened to his arms?" I turned to look back out the open window at Willy flapping his bags wildly after us. I smiled and waved back.

"He fell out of a tree," I said.

"Now, why doesn't that surprise me?" my mother said. She shook her head and smiled.

Willy's parents, as he told me the next afternoon at the pool, were both professors at the local state university. His father was chairman of the psychology department and his mother was an associate professor of economics. He'd brought a pair of sunglasses with him, which he hooked over his regular glasses. To see me clearly he had to lean his head far back so that he could peek out underneath them. His parents, he said, both taught summer school, and so they dropped him off for swim lessons at 7:00 A.M. and he stayed at the pool until 5:00 or 6:00, when they came home again. Some nights he even stayed for the evening swim.

His brain was of constant interest to him. "My IQ is so high," he said, tilting his head way back to watch the new lifeguard leg up into her high chair, "that they can't measure it. I'm off the freak charts. The truth is my dad's having a field day with me, the bastard. Some days I feel like an experiment. Did you know Einstein left home for college when he was just fourteen?"

He asked me what my IQ was, and I told him I didn't know. I had no idea. He turned to look me over then. He rolled his tongue around the inside of his cheek while he measured me up and down. "I'd say you're in the low one-twenties. Frankly, you're lucky. It's just as well. I was talking in phrases at seven months, climbing stairs at eight. And not only is my IQ off the charts, I have a complete photographic memory. I can't forget anything. When I read a book, the paragraphs haunt me at night. I close my eyes and the words scroll down like a goddamned movie or something." He tapped his head. "It's all right here. I'm not bragging. I'm just saying one-twenty-three or so is a pretty good IQ to have if you think about it."

He was also hyperactive. Sometimes he got depressed. "My dad thinks maybe I'm bipolar. He's not willing to grant me manic-depressive status just yet. He says I've got to wait until I grow up to earn that." Willy said he had a psychiatrist of his own, the top guy at the medical school. He talked about dosages of lithium. Drugs were a possibility, he said, but he didn't want them fucking around with his brain. "I've read up on it," he said, "and, frankly those hotshots don't know as much as they think they do about this stuff."

While we were swimming to cool off it came out that Willy, too, was an only child. "Hell, yes," he said, "my mom had her tubes tied when I turned three. They knew what they were in for. They've got their hands full with me and they know it. My parents aren't brilliant, but they aren't stupid either. Why do you think they leave me here all day every day?"

2

Willy's casts came off at the end of July, and when my dad dropped me off at the pool at 8:00 on his way to work, Willy would race to the fence and stand shivering, waiting while I climbed out. My dad and Willy had met, but Dad didn't want to have anything to do with him. "Good morning, Mr. Haley!" Willy would yell, waving wildly. My dad would lean across the seat to look out the window at him. "What's the matter with that young man?" he asked me once. As my dad drove away, Willy would shake his head, looking after the pinked-tight crew cut my dad still wore even though, as a civilian now, his uniform for work was a suit.

"Scary," Willy would say.

That summer we swam and swam, did more than our fair share of time under the lifeguard's chair, tested the limits of the high dive, and spied on the older girls—Joy Baylous, in her white string bikini, and Linda Martin, who had the biggest boobs we'd ever seen. We also played sports, paddleball and tetherball, foosball surrounded by Coke machines in the game room at the pool. Willy had absolutely no talent for physical games, no hand-eye coordination at all, but he would throw himself into them anyway, sweating, spittle flying. "Fuck!" he'd say every time he missed the little paddleball, "*Shit!*"—and he missed it nearly every time.

When we grew tired of the scene at the pool, we caught the bus to see movies downtown, and we spent hours and hours in my backyard firing my Daisy 881 pellet gun into the target of a deer we'd drawn. I had a Case knife my dad had given me for my twelfth birthday, and we practiced throwing it at a stump. Our biggest project was a tree fort that we started far back in the woods behind my house. We'd leave in the morning armed with my dad's hammers and nails and saws and come traipsing back in the late afternoon with bashed thumbs, covered with sweat-stuck sawdust. Then Willy took a leaf of poison ivy and rubbed it up and down his arms. He was awfully smart, but he could be pretty dumb. He wanted, he said, to see what would happen. He thought perhaps he'd built up an immunity to the stuff because of a case he'd gotten on a school picnic two years ago. It turned out he was violently allergic. Within two days the bumps had spread to the tips of his itching fingers and shut down his itching eyes. The doctor sent Willy back to the pool to dry out in the chlorine and sun. He lay stretched out on his towel covered in the pink crust of calamine lotion.

Back in the woods again we discovered the rusty hulk of an abandoned water tank that had been tipped on its side. We climbed inside to sit in it, then relaxed back against the curve of wall with our hands behind our heads, Willy puffing on the Marlboros he swiped one at a time from his dad, while we echoed out possible futures for ourselves. Willy thought he might attend Harvard or Yale and then, perhaps, go on to win a Nobel prize in Physics or something. He said he might want to do that, or maybe he'd be an archaeologist and travel to the Andes, to Northern Africa, Egypt, digging up relics and remains. There were civilizations, he told me, which had yet to be named. He, William Henry Smalls the Third, would name them. I told him I was thinking hard about the Marine Corps—of enlisting when I turned eighteen—I wanted to be a pilot like my dad had been. Since I was a kid I'd had this recurring dream where I was behind the controls of the cockpit of my own jet—hurtling through empty space toward a destination I chose for myself.

Willy blinked back at me. He thumbed his glasses up and shook his head. He snorted out a stream of smoke and flicked away his cigarette. "I don't want to be anything like my father," he said. "How could you want to be anything like your father?"

I picked up a stick and stabbed it in the mud. I shrugged.

One night toward the end of the summer I asked my mother if Willy could come over on Friday and spend the night. Dad wasn't going to be around. He was busier than ever with his new job, leaving early in the mornings now before I got up and not coming home until 7:00 or 8:00. Then sometimes he'd call and say he was going to work late. Weekends, he said—stalwart as the Marine he'd been when I did catch a glimpse of him one night just before bed—weren't an *option*

59

at this point. One night I heard he and Mom talking: there were rumors of layoffs at the plant.

When I asked my mom if Willy could stay, *please*, she pushed the hair out of her eyes and held it against her forehead. "You mean Mr. William Henry Smalls the Third? That," she said, "would be a disaster." In the end, though, she gave in. If his parents consented, she said, Willy could come home from the pool with us on Friday and his parents could pick him up at noon on Saturday morning.

The night started off well enough. Willy thought my mother was the best. "She's too good to be true. She's like that other blonde mom in *Leave It to Beaver*," he said. He followed her around from room to room. He offered to help with dishes, with vacuuming, dusting, anything to ingratiate himself. After we'd eaten pizza and it had grown dark, my mother gave us permission to borrow two of my dad's heavy military flashlights, and we went outdoors to run through the night, having laser wars. It was nearly 9 o'clock when we heard my mother calling us back in. We took our sleeping bags into the den and turned on the television. My dad arrived home at 10:00. We heard the front door unlock and my mom in the kitchen shaking a martini for him. My dad then walked into the den. "Timmy," he said to me and then he looked at Willy. He nodded. "Mr. Smalls," he said. Willy stood up in the too-small Spider-Man pajamas he'd brought to sleep over in and walked over to my dad. He stuck out his hand. "Good evening, sir," he said. They shook hands and my dad went back into the living room to have his drink. Willy rolled his eyes and smiled.

The trouble started sometime deep into the night. I was in my cockpit again, rocketing my plane through space toward a place in my life I'd always wanted to be, when for no apparent reason my engines suddenly burst into flame. I'd been hit, though I'd never seen it coming, and now I was crashing down, engines screaming, toward the ground. I pressed the eject button, but it didn't work.

I woke sitting straight up, my hands gripping the useless controls. The television in the den was fuzzing snow. The rest of the room was dark. Then I looked down and recognized Willy, his mouth cranked wide, his eyes scrunched tight, pink and weak-looking without his glasses, which he took off to sleep, screaming out as if he were the one trapped in the cockpit being burned alive. I grabbed him by the shoulders. "Willy!" I said. "Willy!" But it was too late, the lights upstairs had already flashed on. My mother shadowed into the hallway, gripping her robe closed at the throat. Willy was struggling deep within himself, thrashing back and forth, screaming as if he had been straightjacketed, his arms grappled tight across his chest as if they'd been strapped to him. "No!" he said "No! No! Please!"

"Willy," my mother said calmly, gently. She touched his shoulder, "Willy, wake up."

The soothingness of her voice snapped him out of his deep trance. He looked up at us, stared at my mother and then at me. His grip untensed. His arms relaxed. He let go of himself and his arms slid back. "I had this dream that—" Then he looked down and my mother and I looked where he was looking, at his sleeping bag—a dark piss stain had spread out from his waist. The room reeked of ammonia.

"It must've been all that Coke," my mother said, touching the back of Willy's neck. She went straight to work, trying not to embarrass him. She sent me up to my room for a pair of my pajamas and while I was gone she made the sleeping bag disappear, made up another bed for Willy by laying out the cushions from the couch on the floor. Willy changed in the hall bathroom; my mother told him to leave his pajamas there. She put everything in the washer and started it. Then she waited while we climbed back into our beds. She kissed each of us on the forehead. "Sweet dreams, boys," she said. She turned off the TV and then the light in the hallway and then she started back up the stairs.

I could see Willy's eyes shining in the moonlight.

He saw me looking and rolled over, turning his back to me.

Saturday we waited all morning for Willy's parents to show up. We waited and waited. Noon went by, and then 1:00, 2:00, 3:00, 4:00. We'd watched all the TV we could; we'd been out in the yard; we were supposed to stay close; we couldn't go far. In my room, Willy plopped down on my bed and speed-read Dr. Spock's On Parenting, which had somehow gotten mixed in with the books on my shelves, probably during the move. His forehead shifted down, fully engaged.

"What complete horseshit," he said when he'd finished it, casting it onto the bed.

It was nearly 6:00 when we heard a car pull up in the driveway. Willy ran to the window and looked down into the street. "That's my mom," he said and went tearing out of my room, racing down the hall for the front door. I trailed after him. Mom was in the kitchen fixing dinner.

"Mrs. Smalls is here," I announced and my mom said, "So soon?" but she was grinning.

Willy had beaten the doorbell. He stood in our doorway with the door opened wide. Mrs. Smalls was a chubby little woman with a wired hive of hair. She wore glasses that seemed if possible, even thicker than Willy's.

My mother walked out of the kitchen, wiping her hands on her apron. She put on a smile and reached out her hand and then we all saw what Willy must have seen when he first opened the door. Mrs. Smalls was weeping, her eyes swimming, blurred closed. My mother paused for a second and then she was moving forward, holding out her hands. "Mrs. Smalls," she was saying. I glanced at Willy then, watched the wave of realization pass over his face—later he would tell me it was the actuality of what he'd dreamed the night before. His eyes rolled back in his head and he swooned against the door. He slid down and slumped to the floor.

"Willy!" Mrs. Smalls said.

"Mrs. Smalls," my mother said. "What in the world?"

I stood my ground, rooted there. My mother and Mrs. Smalls helped Willy up, his big alien's head dropping back from his skinny little neck, and carried him down the entranceway to the couch.

3

My mother and I attended the viewing of Willy's father at the local funeral home by ourselves—my dad wouldn't have anything to do with them. Everyone was standing around a red-carpeted room, and Dr. Smalls was on display in his coffin. People would walk past and look at him, paying their last respects. My mother and I took our place in line. I had never in my life seen a real live dead person before. I had never even attended a funeral. I could feel a curious, cold, clammy itch of sweat under my collar. And then it was our turn. Stretched out on a satin blue cloud before us lay Dr. Smalls dressed in a houndstooth sports jacket and black turtleneck. The word was out how he'd hung himself. He'd done it in their bathroom at home using the terry-cloth tie to his robe, knotted it around the iron shower curtain bar anchored firmly in the walls, stood on the toilet and jumped off. "The Bastard," Willy said, "didn't even leave a note." There was no explanation, though as it turned out Willy had known his father was a full-blown manic-depressive—

his father's history of mental health had played significantly into Willy's own early treatment.

Looking down at him lying there then, I couldn't help but notice that Dr. Smalls' head was as big as Willy's, bigger even, if that was possible, and they wore the same type of glasses, the same black-rimmed make and model, the lenses of an equal Coke-bottle thickness. He had his hands crossed comfortably across his stomach, cradling a well-smoked pipe, the stem badly gnawed, the bowl yellowed from use. A cheeriness of rouge had been brushed onto his cheeks, and his thin hair had been Brylcreemed back so that you could see the cold gray gleam of his scalp.

Willy and his mom stood together at the end of the line to accept condolences. Willy was dressed in a blue suit with a red polka-dot clip-on bow tie that had come unhinged and was perched fluttering off to the side like a big butterfly about to take flight. He stood straight up with his feet splayed wide, his hands clasped behind his back, looking even more uncannily like a hair-slicked miniature of his old man. His mother had her handkerchief out and was wheezing into it. As we came by, my mother bent down to hug Willy, but he kept his hands behind his back. He looked past me as he shook my hand.

"My mother and I thank you for your family's concern," was all he said.

4

That fall Willy took a train to a boarding school outside Washington, D.C. I didn't see him again after the viewing, and he never even called to tell me he was going. I imagined that he and his mother had decided the change would be best. Perhaps they felt he couldn't go to school where everyone would know what had happened to him, start out with three strikes against him at a small junior high. The kids would all know about it, they would recall the details of the terry-cloth tie and the leap from the toilet, and they would want to know even more: How does it *feel* to have your father hang himself? Were you *surprised?* Do you think you'll grow up to kill yourself some day too? Willy would have had to suffer their looks, their questions, and the teachers' condolences. Instead he left. Took off on that fast-track Amtrak jet of a train. I tried to see it as if Willy had pulled a Houdini to free himself from the chains of such a bind. He had simply disappeared into thin air. I told myself it was a good trick: he had saved himself. I had to keep telling myself over and over that he hadn't simply abandoned me.

I started school at the local public junior high that fall all by myself again as if I'd never made a friend. Going to school that first morning was like all the other times I'd had to start over in my life. My dad had insisted I begin the year "right"—that I set out dressed for success—and my mother had laid out plaid trousers and loafers, a button-down shirt. That would have been appropriate for the elementary school full up with military brats which I'd attended in Florida, but the kids here were unschooled in such uniform etiquette. They wore whatever they liked, faded jeans and T-shirts, Converse basketball shoes. They stared at me as if I was from the moon, and, indeed, I felt as if I'd just taken that first small step down out of my ship. The girls sniggered and talked behind their books when they saw me in the halls. The boys elbowed each other as I approached and then went silent looking at the ceiling as I walked by.

In my homeroom there were kids named Ezra and Rock, Mona and Mary Lou Anne. I found my seat and sat down. It was a total of two minutes before someone threw the first spit wad. It hit me in the back of the head, and I thought: *Here we go again.*

That afternoon my mother picked me up in the station wagon. As we drove home through town, she asked me how my day had gone. "Great," I said. She smiled and squeezed my knee. "I'm so glad, Timmy." We were silent for a moment and then she said, "Mrs. Smalls called today." I waited and she said. "It's about Willy. He's run away from that school in D.C. She thinks he may try to call you."

I turned to look out the window.

"She doesn't want you to rat him out or anything," my mother continued. "She knows how tight you boys are. But she does want to make sure he's okay. She said to tell him he can come home if he wants. If he's decided he doesn't want to be there. Whatever he wants, she said."

Willy called that night. In the space behind him I could hear a screech of cars, blaring horns.

"It's me," he said.

I asked him where he was.

"I can't divulge that information," he said. "The phone may be tapped. Look, I've only got a minute. A trace takes sixty-six seconds."

"Your mother said you can do what you want. Nobody's tracing anything. She just wants to know how you are."

"Right," he said and laughed. "I'm *nowhere*," he said. "*Everywhere.* I'm right *here.* You know what I'm trying to say?"

"Maybe," I said. "So what now?"

"I don't know. I'm thinking I might try to see a bit of the country. Bum around a bit. I'm kind of at loose ends just now, if you know what I mean. I'm thinking New York City. You ever been there?"

I told him I hadn't. "Look," I said, "you could come back to school here. Maybe it wouldn't be so bad."

There was a long silence. "Time's up," he said and then before I could wish him luck on his journey he clicked off and the line went dead in my hand.

The police found Willy, Mrs. Smalls informed us, an hour later. He'd fallen asleep with his head on the counter of a Dunkin' Donuts in Alexandria, a block and a half away from the gates of the school.

5

That night I took my ship straight up—a rocket shot, seeing the swirling world turning underneath me, let the engines blaze and blaze until they burned out, snuffed, and the jet hung, suspended, turned in space. I reignited, the engines took, and then I blasted back to earth. I came screaming down at Mach 2 toward the blue uprushing ground, and when I pulled her up, just in time, just, it was a miracle the wings didn't yank off, the rivets ratcheting, a miracle I didn't pass out, the gravity jamming my spine small. Nothing worked out; everything did: I *lived*. In fact, with Willy gone, I'd begun to feel that I wouldn't mind seeing a few more places for myself.

When my dad was laid off, we drove all those many miles to California, where he'd taken a job with Boeing. I sat in the middle of the backseat of our station wagon looking out the windshield between my parents, my hands relaxed flat on my knees. We cruised through the bluegrass of Kentucky. Oklahoma was the flattest pancake of a state I'd ever seen. It was amazing how far I could gaze from the raw and windswept peaks of the Rockies. My mother turned and smiled at me. Aviators on, my dad stared straight ahead, negotiating us into the glare. Two days later we caught our first glimpse of the glittering sea, and I couldn't help but think that *here* was right where I was supposed to be. It had to be true, I assured myself. How else could the Mayflower truck find us?

Prison

For B.W.

Fucking queen, I think, fucking snitch, as I walk across the
rec room, watching the queen giggle and blush bright
against his peroxided hair, his daddy, a staring blue eyeball
tattooed across his fat forehead, bending close to whisper in
his ear; while at the other end of the rec room, Wilson's hitting the bag, hitting the bag and not knowing, but me
knowing and listening to him just hit it. Thinking to myself
that if the queen is the sludge at the bottom of this bucket,
then Wilson is the cream at the top, all the rest of these old
convicts and spics and niggers just slopped in.

After three years working this prison, I've learned to
expect the worst from the slop in here and to squash trouble quick. Squash them or they'll squash you, that's my
motto—always knowing that the red button on my hip will
bring a rush of ten other guards if I need them, but I don't
ever need them. I give the queen a look until he knows I

mean it and shuts up. He knows he makes me sick and he knows to shut up when I give him a look. Then glancing over the rest of the rec room I think how it has always kind of reminded me of my old high school gym—and I've always felt good in any gym, even if this one is in a goddamned prison—the rec room's wood floor and the basketball rims all around the sides, the high-up windows and the tall, naked rafters with a bird, who got in somehow though nobody gets out, panicking about between the rafters all day, already maggot ridden in a corner by the next morning, and the walls painted a swimming-pool blue, the old stage set up with guitars and drums and amplifiers, the heavy maroon curtains tied back to the wings, and in and around and over everything the heavy male smells.

It's those smells I'm most familiar with. They give me a good, empty, nervous feel in my gut, the kind of feeling I get when I walk in to a gym to lift, knowing I'm going to push it, kick the shit out of it, but knowing too how much it's going to hurt, how I might throw up or pass out, blackness and a million tingling pins, like I've done before, welcoming it because there's nothing better than pushing that hard. The smells bring it all back to me, not a good smell, but that hard-work smell like the T-shirt you wore under your pads during a tough two-a-day scrimmage in August, bring back that last workout and the anticipation of the next one, that pumped feeling. And it's always the prison smell, the rec room smells of nigger sweat and every colored shade of b.o. from the white Right Guard smell of the old convict types who do nothing more strenuous than play pool all day, down to the spic Columbians who have been in the jungle so long they don't even know what a shower is and who shit standing up on the commode seat because that's the way some joker taught them, that smell of too many men always too close together, that prison smell as constant as damp concrete and the industrial wax from hourly buffed floors, always these prison smells which are the gym smells, that bring it all back to me and make me want to go after it again. So that when I get off, even if I'm working the late shift and I don't get off until twelve at night, I'll stay and lift for two or three hours. I'd lift all day if I could. There's nothing better. So I do this, work in this gym, this prison, and in my spare time I lift.

Snap!

In front of me, five spics are sitting around one of the white, formica-topped card tables, a mushroom cloud of smoke fogged in around their heads, that thick smell of their Padrons edged by too-sweet hair oil. Dominoes lay swirled over the table top, the black edges worn shiny from their fingers, from eight hours of dominoes a day, every day.

Snap!

My eye catches on the new spic who just made his play, flicking his wrist to snap the domino on the table, not quite as sharply as the rest yet, but already learning. He looks up at me but doesn't look away, hunched over with his right hand still resting on the table, his left down between his knees. On his face there's no expression, shark-eyed, his cheeks sharp in to the blade of his nose, his mustache waxed and twirled up to pointy ends, the ragged edge of a badly healed scar from temple to cheek, a lazy eyelid. He just stares at me, black eyes cold and dead.

A sudden clap, I turn to look behind me: a new break, the old convicts are shooting pool at the center table, at the best of the eight tables set in the middle of the room. They think they own the damn place, squatters rights, but I let them know different. Old farts is what they are, hardly better than the spics and niggers.

Wilson catches me with a smile as my eye trails down his way, opposite the stage under the old scoreboard, where the weights are—squat racks and a calf machine and benches and inclines and declines and dip bars and a preacher curl and a pull-up bar and T-bar rowing and barbells and dumbbells. A few niggers and long-haired white guys are pussying around, pretending to work out, pretending to be bad, walking around with their arms out from their sides. Still smiling at me, that damn Bic pen he always chews when he hits the bag turned up out of the corner of his mouth, Wilson nods over at those guys working out. He's seen them too, and I smile back—we're always laughing together at the skinny guys. We laugh at them because we can: there's no points for second place or just for trying, for being third strongest or just half a man—you have to take it all. I'm talking attitude. Wilson knows that and so do I, and we're always laughing at the skinny guys who can't touch us. They don't even come close.

Wilson is one of the blackest niggers I've ever seen, and he's dressed all in white: white tank top, white sweats cut loose at the calf, white wristbands, white socks, and the white Converse high-tops that all the prisoners wear. Dressed all in white, except for a pair of black sunglasses tucked in his waistband. He's shaved down too, not a hair on his body, wearing a light coat of baby oil that glistens over his skin, bunching his muscles tight in the glare of the rec room lights.

"Uncle Swilli," he says to me as I walk up, catching the bag. "I believes His Majesty be at the height of his awesomelyiest hugeness today."

"Shit, Wilson," I say. "You ain't shit." But he is.

Wilson just smiles, whitest damn teeth I've ever seen, flexes a double biceps, long and smooth as swans' necks arching back, and gently kisses them both, pulling each muscle up to his big lips and taking his time with them. "I do believes, Uncle Swilli, that you be jealous of my immense immensity, my universe-sized size, my potential for gargan-tuism."

"Listen Wilson," I say, "you're nothing but a goddamned, skinny-assed Zulu."

Pen in his mouth, he throws his head back and laughs with a breath as big as his expanded chest and goes back to the bag, slaps it quick and hard with the flat of his hand, then starts in again, laughs like that and starts in again not knowing, like he's too big to care, but not knowing . . . *pa-ta-dada pa-ta-dada pa-ta-dada*. . . .

The queen is still sitting over in front of the stage, gig-gling his damn head off. The queen's daddy reaches over and tweaks the queen's balls and the queen giggles again. I look away. We're supposed to stop that shit, but I don't care today. I hope the queen gets gang-banged so I can turn my back on his screams—I could do that much for Wilson—and I think how I'll shake down the queen's cell later, maybe next week, after his browny points waste away, shake down his cell so tight that it'll make what they're doing to Wilson's cell right now seem like an ordinary inspection.

Tap. Tap. Tap. "Testing, testing, one, two, three." Three niggers have climbed up on the stage and have turned on the amplifiers. No one else even bothers to look up, except some other niggers who shamble over to listen close up to the speakers. The guitar squeals and a cymbal crashes.

"Hey, *Po*-lice," the new spic yells at me. He takes his cigar from his mouth and waves it at the niggers tuning their instruments. "Hey, *Po*-lice, you stop them, heh?" he says.

"¿Por que?" I ask as I walk up, throwing my shoulders back and puffing up just a little, just to show him, just play-ing with him.

"Make too much noise. These rap too much noise." He nods and looks at the others and the others nod with him. The spics are all dressed in khakis and white T-shirts, hair slicked back, and the cigars, always the goddamned cigars. The new spic runs a hand through his hair, palm shiny as he takes it away and slides it over his khakis, touches an angry red bump on his chin, smiles, showing off his one gold front tooth. "¿Si?"

I can tell I'm not going to like this new spic. He's too greasy and loud and cocky, the other spics already cowed by him, nodding with him, agreeing with him. I don't like him at all. I know what's going on; he's making a move on me. So I just shrug and turn away—ignoring him, taking him down a peg.

"*Pinga,*" he says. "*Vete al singar.*"

I stop and turn back. The new spic has his foot cocked up on the table, turning a domino in his fingers, weaving it over one finger and under the next. He's just a new spic, and he doesn't know me.

"Excuse me?" I say and for long seconds it hangs like that between us, not backing down, and I can feel it rushing through me, tight in my arms, that blood pumping me to my full size, and I'm just ready to go off, to squash him—I don't even consider the button, this spic's mine, and to rule this gym I have to make him mine, take him by myself, he's mine—and I'm on the edge, cool as stone inside, so cool inside I could laugh and grab him by the throat, just waiting for him to make the first move so I won't get fired, so I can fire off the line, come on, I'm thinking, come on, come on you fucking spic; until one of the others leans up and touches the new spic's foot.

"No, Policia," he says and looks up from the new spic to me and smiles. "Hah, joke," he says. Then all the spics are smiling, and I smile too with my lips tight together, then all the spics are laughing, a great joke, a game of chicken, a dare, and it's over just that quick.

The niggers start up with their three chords, and giving

the new spic a last hard stare, a promise, I let it go for now. I've got other things on my mind, and he's not going anywhere.

The spics start slapping down the dominoes even sharper, sharper and louder than the high crying notes of the lead guitar, the slow train-whine of the harmonica, and with the music the whole volume of the place seems to rise, the *snap* of the dominoes, a new break, the crash of a barbell to the floor, the steady time of Wilson on the bag, steadier than the drum.

Every song they know, I know by heart, this one Muddy Waters's "Manish Boy," and everyone else knows these songs too, except the new spic, and he'll learn; being here every day, he'll learn. I'm thinking how I'll teach him to learn.

"Hey, Sonny," one of the old convicts says and waves me over to the pool tables in the middle of the room. I walk over slowly, start to ask him what he wants, but the convict holds up the flat of his hand while his partner lines up a shot, leaving me there with my arms crossed over my chest. His partner bends down and squints, stands up and chalks his cue, baby-powders his fingers, slides the stick over them, smoothes the powder in his palm and up and down the cue, bends again and squares his legs and squints, his old forehead wrinkling up, arches his hand, and backspins the cue ball with a short, quick follow-through into the three, which slides into the side pocket, the cue ball rolling back and leaving him with a follow on the seven.

Only then does the old convict look at me, like I was waiting outside his office—but it's my gym. He's nothing. Nothing but an old man. His eyes are milky blue, like a blind man's eyes. He's been here forty years and looks more like a guard than most of the old guards look.

"Hey, Sonny," he says and puts his hand on my shoulder,

squeezes my traps, tries to do it a little too hard, but he's nothing; I could laugh. "Can't you do something about them niggers?" He looks at me. "I mean goddamn," he says. Looking over at the niggers, he frowns and shakes his head. "You know what I mean? Tough shot," he says as his partner sinks the seven in the far corner pocket and lines up the thirteen. "Niggers," the convict says again and shakes his head, his eyes are sad and tired but glued to his partner. "Nice shot, Lou. Goddamn worse every year. The niggers, I mean. Ain't they worse, Lou?" Lou doesn't answer; he's working an angle on the one.

"Why don't you tell them to stop then, Franky?" I say. I'm standing there, and I'm really tired of his shit, just fucking tired of it. He stops with his jaw set.

"Listen, Sonny," he starts, "if I was. . . ."

I just turn away, leaving my back wide open to him, flexing my lats wide, feeling my shirt spread tight. He's nothing. One time he might have been, but now he's nothing, and I just turn away, leave him with his mouth full of things he did and can't do anymore, leave the old men to their pool. Wandering away from the pool tables, I take it slow and easy, cool, back into the center of the rec room, the song pulsing in my ears.

The queen is whispering now, whispering and giggling, giggling and primping, giggling with his hand at his mouth, and his daddy eating it up, smiling as he rocks back in the chair, his forehead wrinkling, making the eyeball wink. I'm short, the queen explained to me the day before, cheeks flushed, only three months to go. He said Wilson was going to get caught running the stuff sooner or later and he didn't want to take the chance of their whole block getting busted. Told me the dope is on a string of dental floss hung out of Wilson's Plexiglas window; and that's where I told Wilson's unit officer to find it. That's my job; I did my job. But I

wouldn't have gone looking for it, not in Wilson's cell. Goddamn queen. Wilson taking a fall from a homo, not a man in
this prison would dare it, not even me, but to this woman,
a sneaky-ass homo. . . .

Behind me the convicts are racking them up again, the
spics keep slapping the dominoes, the bag going *pa-ta-dada
pa-ta-dada*. I can feel it, the hair prickling up on the back of
my neck, the new guy watching me again, challenging me.
I watch him back, the fucking skinny-assed spic. Who in
the hell does he think he is? I'll break his fucking neck. He
doesn't take his eyes off me as I walk toward him, and I don't
take mine off him, not for a second, giving it to him all the
way up to the table.

"You want something?" I say, and I've got my shoulders
back, my arms crossed over my chest, and I know how big
I am in front of him.

He just stares at me with those black eyes, cold and dead.
And it's then, looking down at him as he leans back from the
table, that I see his left hand's gone, sheered away at the
wrist, notice too his tattoo, and I wonder I didn't notice it
before, a black splotch of ink between the first finger and
thumb of his right hand. It's really a tattoo over a tattoo, the
old one scribbled out by a newer blotch of green ink, hiding what was there, burying the symbol, the tiny heart
stuck with the sickle of the executioner or the five dots of
the habitual criminal, and suddenly I know where this new
spic's been. A Marielitos. I've heard the stories, and I imagine what he's been through, the lost hand, the scar, the lazy
eyelid. I've heard the stories of those prisons, but this is the
first time I've ever seen a man who's been all the way to the
end of the line.

"¿Que es eso?" I ask him, pointing at the blotched tattoo, though I already know what it is, where he's been to
get it, and just knowing it puts this guy in a different

league, on a new level, and I'm wondering what the hell he did to get here.

Not saying anything, his tongue works the inside of his cheek, thinking what it might cost him to answer. "Cuba," he says finally, thickly accented, inspecting the blot of tattoo himself as he rubs at his thin ear with the nub of his wrist, kind of melted over so the bone doesn't show. That's all he says. But he looks at me, his eyes cold and gone away, and whatever he sees in me looking at him starts to crack at the corners of his face, and then he laughs, laughs at me, laughing without laughter, loud and obviously at me, and I feel it flush up hot into my face, and his teeth are rotten and brown, the one gold tooth winking obscenely, and I smell his breath from deep down inside his rotting guts, laughing and the skin tight on his face with his laughing, shrunken to his skull, still laughing, and it shivers through me, but I don't show it. You can't show it. Squash them or they'll squash you, I tell myself. Tell myself, he'll own you if you let him. Fuck his laughter. Fuck where he's been. Fuck him. His feet are on the table and I give them a good swift kick off onto the floor just to show him.

The Cuban stops laughing and looks at me and then he's on his feet. The other spic stands up between us and says something in Spanish too quick for me to understand, and the Cuban shoves the little spic aside, knocking him over a chair which scrapes back and smacks sharply to the floor. Around us the others are watching, the music stops, leaving us face to face in a sudden ring of silence. The Cuban is touching his pants, fingering the seam down his thigh, and I see the quick light as he flicks the razor blade out from its hiding place. I take a step back, just out of his reach. My hand hovers over the red button, but I don't touch it. Everyone is watching now, and I have to take him by myself. He's mine. Everyone's watching, and I have to take him. The

Cuban's face is shiny, skinny, sharp, spittle caking the corners of his mouth, rabid-like, insane, eyes dark and hard and mean, and I can see he's too far gone to even know about being afraid any more, not afraid of using that razor, or of the consequences of using that razor, knowing he'll use it. And right then, before it's even really begun, I know I've already lost, letting him get off the line with that razor between his fingers, and almost without knowing it, I'm reaching for the button, but I can see him tensing, inching up, watching my throat, and I know I'll be dead before I can touch it. For a second it can go either way, but he's standing there with that razor blade and nothing in his eyes, crazy as hell, and I drop my hand from the button, turn on my heels and walk away, my hands shaking and legs warm-weak.

"Adios, *maricon*," he says, clear, not loud, but clear. I don't stop. I'm telling myself to turn around, turn around, but I don't. I keep walking, walk away, tell myself to push the button, but I don't, and everyone still watching and quiet, but I keep my head up, fixing my eyes on a dark blue spot on the back wall.

Then the pool balls go back to clacking, the dominoes snap, the band begins in the middle of the same endless three-chord song. But they don't look at me. No one will look me in the eye, ignoring me as if I wasn't even there. Wilson looks at me, though, chokes the bag off at the throat and looks at me as I come close, wearing his big, white-toothed, nigger smile.

"What's the matter, Uncle Swilli?" he says with a look over at the Cuban then back at me. "You look like you seen a ghost." He's laughing at me, that goddamned pen still in his mouth. "I ain't afraid of no ghost," he says.

I'm standing in front of him, and I hear the old convicts laughing too, and I know what they're saying, Wilson still smiling, smiling at me like we both used to smile at the skinny asses, except now he's smiling at me. And I think, you fucking nigger, you goddamned, fucking nigger, you ain't nothing but a nigger—then it hits me. I glance down at my watch. Then I give it to him like he deserves it, cold and sharp as a blade.

"About time you were heading back to your cell, isn't it, Wilson?" I ask him. I ask him cool and so calm. *Jesus,* I'm calm. I almost scare myself I'm so calm.

He looks up at the big scoreboard clock then at me, puzzled. "No, man, I still gots to pump the iron and run a few. You knows I'm in the permanent business of developing this mythological physique to new heights of awesominity." He smiles, but I don't.

"Yeah," I say and leave him there, the bag silent behind me, and when I stop by the pool tables and glance back he's still staring after me. Our eyes meet. He fumbles at his waist then slides his sunglasses on, goes back to the bag. And hearing it, I can smile, catching that extra stutter, that off-time in his beat, I want to laugh, watching until he misses and the bag spins around, around and around on the hook, Wilson not bothering to touch it, wiping the trickling sweat from his face as he studies his white shoes, touches those black glasses. He looks at the locked gate.

At the table, the Cuban snaps down his domino, catching on, and he glances up at me but not away, the queen laughs, shrill and high, hysterically, and the pool balls break and scatter for the pockets, the niggers play their three chords and sing, and Wilson starts to beating up the bag again, but his timing's off and it isn't going to come back. I'm never going to let it. And I take a good deep breath of the gym air, feel the blood pump full and tight and hard into my arms with those strong smells—can't wait to hit the iron when I get off work. I want to hurt and tingle, kill myself to show these fuckers what the iron is all about, what the weights mean. It's an attitude. And with that good feeling in me, I smile at the Cuban and wink: All right mister, all right, fuck where you've been and your razor blade. I'll ride you the rest of the way down that line. I'll ride you all the way. Mouthing to him, *You're mine, baby, you're mine.*

Jackie

Jackie sat at a table by the windows that overlooked Perdido Beach smoking a Marlboro, waiting while Steve made the margarita she'd ordered. The only other customer at the Reef—a golf type, wearing a white visor, bright-pink, coral-colored polo shirt and khaki shorts—rested the weight of both of his hairy forearms on the bar, smoking and drinking a draft while watching football news on ESPN. Steve Foley stood behind the bar in his Wash Up At THE REEF for Happy Hour! T-shirt, whirring the blender. It was just after 2:00 on a September Thursday afternoon—the 23rd—early yet for the fliers from the airbase in Pensacola, and the summer kids in their bathing suits and flip-flops who spilled loudly out onto the deck all summer long had gone back to their respective colleges. Steve kept the bar he owned dark, air-conditioned cool against the bright, eighty-three-degree day—fall for northern Florida. Through the bank of tinted windows before which Jackie sat, the ocean shone an eerie, shark-shimmering, metallic blue against the starkly glowing gold-green sands of the Gulf.

Steve set the margarita in front of Jackie, shielding it with his left hand. He'd topped the thick, icy slush of her drink with a single pink candle. "Happy birth-day," he sang in the lilt of his sort-of brogue—Irish from South Boston—"to you," and then, seeing he'd surprised her, he grinned out from behind his red tangle of beard.

Jackie sat back, touched. She tucked her hair behind her ears. "How did you know it was my birthday?" She hadn't reminded the girls at the shop, The Limited, at the mall in Orange Beach, where she was the manager, and none of them had remembered. She hadn't told anyone, though she'd been consciously carrying the fact of this day, her coming birthday—her *thirtieth* birthday—inside her for weeks, since the end of August, which had signaled the end of summer on the calendar, even though it was still too hot to believe summer was gone, fall begun, if you'd grown up where she had, in the leaf-blazing, tree-full mountains of West Virginia. Today was her thirtieth birthday, but Thursdays were her regular day off, and she'd done what she always did on Thursdays during the summer, relying on the routine that she'd honed to help her through this day too.

She woke in her queen-sized bed to the alarm at 6:45 with Max, her big yellow lab, stretched out snoring deeply beside her, and dressed in gray sweatpants and an old V-neck T-shirt for a half-hour walk along the stretch of beach that fronted the one-bedroom condominium she owned in the Seafarer. Max raced beside her, chasing seagulls, rushing into the surf again and again barking after a stick she threw. Back in her third-floor condominium, tasting the salt from the sea mixed with a slight sweat on her lips, she filled a glass of water from the tap and scrolled open the blinds to let in the sun, her sideways view of the wide ocean. Then she made coffee, fed Max his two cups of Purina Dog Chow, and changed his water. Max lapped at it vigorously, the metal bowl ringing against the imitation tile floor.

In the shower, she soaped and shaved her legs. With a towel wrapped around her, she repainted her toenails, red. The college-aged girls at the store who worked for her were painting their nails silver, dark purple, or even black, the fashion these days, but Jackie couldn't help but think that it made them all look like aliens. The black one-piece bathing suit she'd bought last year hung where she'd left it to dry on the doorknob, and she lifted it off and stepped into it, slid the straps over her shoulders. Finally, she tucked her long black hair up under a Braves baseball cap and put the book she'd been reading all summer—a water-stained and suntan-oiled paperback copy of Tolstoy's *Anna Karenina*—into her bag. She was making herself ignore all the current best-sellers until she was through, though she was still only on page 273. "Stay off the couch," she scolded Max, who was at the door looking up at her, wagging his tail, hoping to go, and closed and locked the door behind her.

She spent her day off lying on her big towel on the beach, intermittently reading and catnapping. Only a few other people were out, mostly walkers, older folks who flocked to Florida each fall, who passed her, nodding or waving, saying, "Nice day!" and continued on. She took a dip in the condo's pool. No one else was at the pool but Billy, the bone-thin maintenance man with the bushy side-whiskers, who had to wear a fist-sized, flesh-colored hearing aid, and who reminded Jackie of her father back in Nitro—the little town in West Virginia where she'd grown up. Billy grinned at her, "Hello there, Jackie!" as he bent to empty the skimmers. A wind gusted off the water, almost cool, and she wrapped herself in the towel and turned her back to the breeze, hold-

ing the towel tight with her elbows, and tried to light a cigarette with a flip of her Zippo. She inhaled deeply, dropped
the lighter back in her bag, and dragged a white plastic
lounger into the sun. Still wrapped in the towel, she laid
back and fished out her book.

At 1:00 she collected her things. In the shower this time,
she washed her hair. Women who came into the dress shop
often eyed her hair; it was that black, without a hint of
brown or a single shimmer of red, or the gray roots from
needing to be dyed again. But Jackie didn't color it. She did
have to use a ton of conditioner, went through nearly a bottle a week, because she chose to wear it long and straight.
Dresses were her business—The Limited carried all of the
latest styles, the fall line adorning the mannequins in the
front windows—and Jackie, as manager, was expected to
wear these clothes, though she steered away from miniskirts
and high boots—left these things to the girls who worked
the floor. Her closet, though, was surprisingly bare. Mostly
long, dark skirts and sensible shoes. Silk blouses in black or
white or red. A jacket of some sort when she could get away
with it. Jackie always felt frozen in the store, hugging herself over the sweater she left at her office. In summer the
mall cranked up the air conditioner for the comfort of their
customers power-walking the halls. When she walked outside at the end of her day, she was always glad to greet that
first wet wave of heat smelling of the sea that bathed her the
moment she stepped into the parking lot.

From the organized display in her bedroom closet, Jackie
picked out an ankle-length, summer madras garden-party
dress—she'd had it for years—but Steve Foley had once
remarked how "pretty" she looked in it. She allowed herself to take the new sandals she'd bought from the store—a
gift for herself—out of the box and to unwrap them from
the tissue paper. She buckled them on and stood before the

full-length mirror on the back of her bedroom door. It always surprised her. If she caught a glance of herself or let herself look long enough into her own face, she *was* her mother. She switched the pack of Marlboros and lighter from the beach bag into her purse and took the red lipstick, which she normally wore only at work, and drew it on her lips in the pink, shell-shaped mirror beside the front door before dropping it into the purse. Then she took the elevator down to the parking lot. Each condo had its own carport; hers was number eleven. She climbed in to her nondescript, no-nonsense Escort and drove herself to the Reef.

"Jackie," Steve said, tisking her. He shook his head. "How did I *know* it was your birthday? How could I *forget?* Now, blow it out before it melts your drink."

Jackie bunched her hair back and leaned to the flame.

"Wish!" Steve said.

Jackie waited. Then she took a breath and blew close. The flame danced away from her, then snuffed out, the smoke rising in a long curlicue, ghosting blue-gray against the darker walls, the dot of the wick aglow. She took the candle out of the drink and set it on the napkin. She raised the frosted glass to Steve.

"And many many more to you, lass," he said and bent and kissed her on the cheek.

Jackie watched Steve as he walked back to the bar, smiled despite herself. The golf type had turned to watch. "Happy birthday, beautiful." He raised his beer. He had on one of those big, lunky, silver watches and a clunky, gold college ring. He was eyeing her up and down, grinning, and Jackie caught Steve's eye. One reason she drank at the Reef—actually it was the only place she drank, certainly the only bar where she would ever consider going to have a drink by herself—was that Steve didn't let any of the men hassle her. She could come here on her day off, take a break from being in her little place without going anywhere near a mall, and sit at a table and have a cold glass of Chablis or an occasional margarita in the early afternoon and enjoy the sight of the ocean along with the first relaxing glow of the alcohol, which allowed her to remain both privately inside of herself and outside of herself in a public space at the same time. Jackie had always felt safe at the Reef. She turned back to the tinted view of the Gulf, the companionship of her cigarettes and her drink.

"What's *her* problem?" she heard the man say—his voice slightly slurred—and heard Steve reply for her, without her having to say one word, "My guess is that she's trying to enjoy her drink alone, friend. Why don't you try to enjoy yours?"

Thirty.

God.

The talk-show talk was that age didn't matter anymore—you were as young as you felt, as young as you wanted to feel—but just then Jackie felt how significant the day was, the years were. She was thirty. Thirty now. And even if she didn't look thirty, even if she could get away with saying she was twenty-seven until she turned thirty-two, maybe even thirty-three, she was thirty. The truth was worse: she *felt* thirty. There was no escaping that fact—no escaping the facts. Certainly it wasn't too late for her to have a baby, but her biological clock was definitely ticking away. Ever since she'd been a child herself, Jackie had pictured herself with children of her own someday. She'd wanted babies and had simply always assumed she'd have them when she met Mr. Right. But she had not met Mr. Right. Now she was thirty, and the life she'd always imagined for herself as a matter of course was not her life.

She'd been twenty—a baby herself, she thought, from the perspective of her seat before the view of the Gulf looking back at her life from the age of thirty now—when she'd moved to Pensacola. It had been mid-November then, her twentieth birthday already almost two months past. She'd simply left, had not even bothered to drop her classes at that college, forsaking the scholarship she'd earned and taking Fs in all five courses in which she'd been enrolled. When people asked her where she'd gone to school, she didn't name that school. She told them Nitro, where she'd graduated from high school. Sitting, smoking before the picture of the beach at the Reef, she was left wondering at the person she'd been then. Who had she been as that girl—the core of the woman she felt herself to be at thirty now? But the decisions that girl, that baby, had made had shaped her into who she was sitting before the tinted windows of the Reef today, smoking and drinking by herself to celebrate the thirtieth year since her birth.

For the second time that day, Jackie thought about her mother, who'd died of the cancer which had begun in her left breast when Jackie was in junior high school. Would her life have turned out differently if she'd had a mother to run home to that morning? Someone she could have told? She saw the bruising of her mother's face, that sink of her cheeks as her life was sucked away, her skin pasted whiter against the white pillow, the heavy-dark circles under her eyes, that tiredness, all of her own beautiful black hair lost to her—along with her breasts. By then, she'd had both of them removed, the right breast, too, just to be safe. But that hadn't saved anything. She died during Jackie's senior year.

At the time of her mother's death, Jackie had been dating a boy named Jake. Jake and Jackie: Jackie and Jake. She was seventeen; he was nineteen. Before her mother died, Jackie had had the notion that she would remain a virgin for her husband-to-be. Jackie wasn't entirely sure where she'd gotten this strong notion—it hadn't come from church, which she attended sporadically at best, certainly not from her parents' warnings, they didn't try to scare her, they didn't threaten or even impose a curfew, they trusted her to do what she felt was right, that was the word her mother used, "trust"—but she was fully aware that she was *proud* of her resolve, and strong enough always to put a stop to things when the petting with Jake got too hot. It wasn't about "purity." She was perfectly in control.

These were the sorts of conversations they had: sitting at the kitchen table after school in the afternoons over burnt-tasting cups of coffee sweet with sugar and milk, her mother told her she had been a virgin for Jackie's father, though, her mother was quick to add with a laugh, she wasn't sure she'd wait again for him to have sex the first time. She and her mother had always spoken that frankly about her life. When Jake and Jackie had dated for over a year, it was Jackie's mother who suggested that perhaps Jackie should go on the pill. But then her mother had died, and they'd put her in a black shiny coffin and buried her. Three nights after the funeral, Jackie asked Jake to make love to her, told him her wish through the press of her hips against his hardness, her tongue in his mouth, helping him take off her bra, her skirt, his shirt, the buckle on his belt jingling. Through the hurt, she'd hardly felt any pain, though the pain was certainly there. She'd bled onto the skirt, a slash of deep, rusty red, which would have been an impossible thing to hide from her mother's eyes, but which her father hadn't even thought to notice, especially under the circumstances. At the end, when Jake had come, his whole body spasming his love, she'd been left crying in his arms, sobbing. Jake thought it was from the hurt, her sadness of losing her virginity, her resolve—of something he'd done *to* her—and he held her close, their bodies pulsing together on the sticky backseat of his father's old Galaxie 500, and stroked her hair and said he was sorry, he was so sorry, he loved her, he loved her, over and over, until she'd wrung it all out of herself. She fixed her eyes and lips in the rearview mirror. Then Jake drove her home. She tied her sweater around her waist and walked past her father, who was sitting in the family room watching TV zombielike, drinking a sixth beer, the empty cans of Pabst Blue Ribbon adding up on the counter. Jackie never explained to Jake. That moment was hers—her *living* moment: *life*. She was still *alive*. It was something Jake could never have understood—his mother and father were walking around, talking, giving orders, delineating boundaries, offering advice; he wasn't equipped for the kind of understanding Jackie had been forced to know. Not that she wished it on him; it was simply not something she cared to share with Jake—or anybody else, for that matter. Knowing about that kind of love was earned knowledge that was hers alone. Sometimes, still—*right then*—sitting by herself at the Reef—Jackie could miss her mother so much, it felt as if someone had blown a hole through her.

Her father, Ira, still worked in the train yard for Union Carbide. Nitro, the name of the little town on the Kanawha River where she told people she'd grown up, was explosive enough. The name always got a laugh. But worse were the jokes they always suffered because of the sulfur smoke from the Carbide plant chugging out of the factory stacks poking up everywhere, the dingy yellow stink of it mushrooming into the sky—the match scratch smell of it deep down in the flowered fabric of their couches and chairs, coloring the walls of their ranch-style two-bedroom house (sitting there at the table at the Reef, a thousand miles away, she could smell it still as pungently as if she were a girl of eight sitting back home beside her father before their old, black-and-white Victrola TV) and didn't it have to be in their lungs, their skin, their hair, livers, kidneys, breasts? Always wondering, she'd always wondered, if that seeping burnt chemical smell hadn't contributed to her mother's death. Of course, Jackie strongly suspected that it was in her as well—the writing on the wall—the future of her own death foretold in her mother's—she'd been born and raised in that atmosphere. She was her mother's daughter. Naked, nightly, before she stepped into the shower, she inspected each of her breasts, the right one a bit smaller, the left with a dark brown mole on the aureole, both pillowy soft and maddeningly cystic. She was scared to death of what they might be hiding, as if the 34C-size of them might be loaded: *Nitro!* Since watching her mother die, she'd pictured herself in that same hospital bed, her mother as herself, bald, her own black hair fallen out from the chemo, her own left arm bloated too big to belong to her, she as her mother, her mother as herself—wouldn't she die like that, too? At thirty, even though she was careful to check herself nightly and to have herself examined yearly, it was still a premonition that haunted her life. Back then, every weekend when they met, home from a week at their separate colleges at opposite ends of the state—Jake had gone to the state university in Morgantown, while Jackie, as salutatorian of her high school class, had accepted a President's Scholarship at the state university in Huntington—she and Jake would hike up into the hills to lay flowers—white daisies—on her mother's grave. Daisies, Jackie found, were the only flower that would live until their return with fresh flowers the following week.

And then Jake stopped coming home to meet her. One weekend he said he had to work on a group project for marketing; the next he had to study for a midterm in biology. There was, he finally admitted on the phone when she called him on it, another girl. Her name was Trina. But he would always love her, Jackie. He just couldn't do "the long-distance relationship thing anymore." He wanted them, he said, to "stay friends." He would "always be there for her."

Jackie cried in her dorm room for two days, missing classes and meals, though she couldn't say exactly what she was crying about. She didn't think it was all about Jake, certainly it was for loss—her losses. She had never been sure she *loved* Jake—not if love, or at least some common denominator of the foundation for what could be called love, was what she knew she felt for her mother. She recognized the foundation of that feeling, charged as it was by desire for a boy. But she felt sad about losing Jake's professed love. It all made her feel so alone again, left behind; Jackie recognized the symptom as grief. Then her roommate, Lanier, from Matewan, who had been sneaking oranges and rolls out of the dining hall for her, convinced her to go out with her. "Screw him," she said. "That jerk Jake. He's a dickhead. Let's *party!*" In the weeks and months since she'd arrived at college, Jackie hadn't stayed around town to go out on weekends with the other girls on her floor. Now she did. The legal drinking age was eighteen, and they went to all the places where they could get a drink, the places where the boys were drinking. They got dressed in their Jordache jeans and they did their hair up big and went to the bars and to the dance clubs, Verbs and the Mad Hatter. During the week, the fraternities on campus held parties, *Jifs,* they called them, after T.G.I.F.s. During the week, Jackie and her friends went there. It had been at one of these Jifs, a month or so after Jake had broken up with her, that Jackie had first seen the tall, sandy-haired boy the other boys called Jeb because his real name was Stuart. She hadn't gotten it at first.

Jackie looked down. Her cigarette was out. She stubbed it into the ashtray, shaking her head at herself—at the idea of her smoking. She hadn't smoked back then, in college, would never have touched a cigarette in high school. The loss of her virginity and the taking up of smoking, the two things she swore she'd never do as a girl, were perhaps the best two outward mile marks of her journey into young womanhood. She'd taken up the habit after she'd left that college and moved here, within a few days of accepting the job at the dress shop. Most of the other sales girls smoked during their breaks while hanging out together among the fake fronds under the skylight in the middle of the mall. Smoking was the sign that you belonged to their group. But even then, at twenty, when Jackie had started, smoking a cigarette during her morning break with one or two of the other girls, maybe one during lunch, and then another in the evening at home alone after dinner, three a day, she would never have believed she'd still be smoking at *thirty*. She would never have believed that some days she could smoke an entire pack, and, on the tense day when she had to puzzle together the weekly work schedule for the dozen or so girls who worked at the store, a pack and a half. Smoking was a dumb thing to do, and Jackie knew she wasn't dumb. If breast cancer didn't claim her, lung cancer would. *What did she think she was doing?* Tomorrow she would quit, she decided, and recognized the feeling of resolve. But not yet. Not today. She reached for her purse, the pack of Marlboros and her lighter. She lit another cigarette and set the lighter flat on the table. She took that first sweet drag and blew it away from herself, over her shoulder. Jackie sipped her drink.

When she finished her margarita, Steve brought her another one. She reached for her purse to pay for it.

"Jackie," Steve said disappointedly and put his hands on

his hips. "It's your *birth*-day. Now," he said, eyeing her, "tell the truth. In all these years, I've never asked. How old are you anyway?"

As if she'd been carded, Jackie pulled out her Florida driver's license and handed it to him. In the ten years since she'd moved, the license had expired and been renewed twice. The picture showed her as she was: a pretty, green-eyed girl with a mane of raven-black hair. The day she'd had the picture taken she'd been wearing a white silk blouse from the store; she'd stopped by the Department of Motor Vehicles on her way to work. She had on bright-red lipstick—the same shade she was wearing today. The license gave her vital statistics: Born 9/23/68; Eyes: Green; Ht: 5' 6"; wt. 123. She was an organ donor. In case of an untimely death, she'd signed over her organs to be used to help someone else to live. It had scared her to sign that release—the flutter of it inside her giving flight to the life still beating in her heart—but she'd been proud to have signed it, too. She'd thought of her mother, and for a moment she'd felt *brave*. Steve handed the license back to her.

"Thirty? Is that why you look so glum? Thirty's not old!" Steve smiled, looking mischievous, boyish, decidedly not-old, even though she knew he was forty-five. "Some days, you know, when the college kids are here in their baggy shorts, listening to that rap, I get to feeling I'm a fossil. I know I was like them way back when—it was the seventies, I must have been, right?—even though I'd been drafted— but I can't really remember it at all. Not like they're living it. There now, see? You should think of this as a sort of *graduation* from your twenties. Mother Mary! My twenties! My *thirties!*" Steve shook his head. "Now Sam is turning *twelve!*" Sam, *Samantha,* was Steve's red-haired and prettily freckled daughter. "Turning thirty is something to celebrate!

You don't have to go through your twenties again. Praise the Lord! You and me, Jackie, we're *mature*. Thank God!"

"Hey, buddy," the golfer guy in the visor cap called from his seat, tapping the filter end of a cigarette against the bar. "Hey, pal. Isn't this a bar? Why do I have to wait why you get to flirt with that gorgeous girl?" Jackie noticed for the first time that the man was trying to grow a mustache. A shudder ran up her spine: it looked as if one of those hairy-looking centipede bugs that she often found by the drain in her bathtub when she got up to take a shower in the mornings had been caught and squashed by his nose while trying to scuttle away into the more shadowy aspects that combined to shape his face. The man saw her looking and winked.

Steve thumbed over his shoulder and smiled sweetly for Jackie while saying loudly enough for the man to hear, "Excuse me while I serve this asshole who's trying hard to get himself punted out into the street."

He left the gift of the second drink and turned back to his job. Jackie smoked now and sipped her second margarita and looked out at the glowing ocean. Behind the Reef a jetty jutted far out into the shallow Gulf. A shrimper skirted by—gulls flocking the hanging net.

Jackie watched Steve as he worked behind the bar and had to admit there was something in the way he walked that had always interested her. Steve was tall, lanky-strong, with the strength of blue veins mapping his freckled arms. He had slim hips and wide shoulders, wore a uniform of dark-blue Levis and clean construction boots, his graying hair—penny-dulled from a once-brilliant Irishy red to merely coppery—curled to the collar of his T-shirt. Steve had owned the Reef, where he'd started work as a bartender in his twenties after his discharge from the service, since he'd turned thirty himself, so giving up his twenties had been a sort of graduation for him, too. Just last month, he'd had another sort of graduation. He'd finally obtained the divorce he'd been seeking since he'd turned forty. The divorce proceedings had dragged on for five years and had been, in his words, "bloody awful." His wife, Sally, had had a series of affairs, and Steve, in order to get sole custody of Samantha, which he was absolutely determined to do, had had to go through the official mess of proving through a detective agency what everyone in the small town of Perdido already knew for sure about her; photographs of her with her lovers—including one of Steve's closest friends, not to mention their family pediatrician, a man with four kids himself—motel reservations, times and dates, the length of every afternoon assignation, the whole lurid mess.

Another trial for Steve had been that though he and his wife had been officially separated during the entire time it had taken to prove his case, he hadn't been able to see anyone else for fear Sally had hired a detective of her own. He hadn't wanted to give her any chance of leveraging their daughter away from him. "I'm thinking about giving up the bar and becoming a priest, what do you think?" he'd joked, the strain of his forced celibacy in the tight stretch of his smile. In all the time she'd known him, Jackie had never seen Steve with another woman. He reached for the tap. "Yes, sir, right away, sir," he said, "another cold Miller Lite coming right up, sir."

Steve was okay. He really was. When she'd first arrived in Pensacola, Jackie had waitressed at the Reef through the winter months before the job she'd applied for at the dress shop had come through. She'd applied for the afternoon shift at the Reef advertised in the local *Gazette,* the shift none of the other waitresses wanted in the off-season because business was as slow as it was today—the Reef didn't serve much of a lunch, burgers and dogs, frozen fries, steamers. Jackie, on the other hand, refused to work nights. "Hey," Steve said, "That works for me. You're hired." He even went so far as to lend her two hundred dollars against her first check. He hadn't known her from Adam—or Eve, for that matter—but he'd rung open the register right then and asked how much she needed. "Are you all right?" he asked. "Are you okay?" looking into her eyes. And he hadn't been coming on to her. He was just being *Steve*. He owned a fishing boat, *The Reefer*, and some weekends after she'd begun working there she went out with him and Samantha and some of the other waitresses and bartenders, a few loyal customers and friends of Steve's—even back then, ten years ago, his wife, Sally, had always refused to go. She said she got seasick. Instead, she took tennis lessons at the club; there was a new pro. Jackie sat beside Samantha in the tall tower—she and Samantha were buddies, "the girls" they called themselves, as in "The girls would like another Coke, please, Steve," and "The girls would like to swim"—while Steve stood against the rail and searched the bright haze of horizon with binoculars for the marlin that made their home in the Gulf. Steve loved deep-sea fishing, but when Jackie went out with them he seemed content to sit with her and Samantha and captain "the girls" through the blue ocean and drink beer, his second favorite thing to do, Ipswich Ale or Bass Ale or Harpoon iced freezing cold in two coolers big enough to keep two big fish fresh and firm, grouper even. Yes, Jackie had to admit she was interested in Steve and she genuinely cared about Samantha—she listened to Sam talk about her mother, knew enough from the friend her own mother had been to her to know that listening was all that was expected of her—but even in the weeks since he'd been safely divorced, nothing had ever happened between Jackie and Steve. They'd remained what they'd

97

always been, friends; she knew all about the pain his divorce had caused him, and she'd told him all about the death of her mother.

In the ten years since she'd left college, given up her Presidential Scholarship and taken her Fs and told her father she was leaving school (Her reasons were concrete enough to seem real—she wasn't cut out for academics; she wanted to go where it was warm; she was tired of school; she didn't have any friends; she wanted to get out in the world and earn a living—generic, harmless-seeming explanations that ended with Jackie in tears, sobbing uncontrollably, hysterically, while her father held onto her, soothing her, patting her hair as he held her, whispering to her calmly as if he were talking a horse out of a barn fire, "Whatever you want to do, Jackeline. It's your life, honey. That's what your mama would want for you, I'm sure."), since then there had been a few guys—all disasters. She had tried. She had forced herself to try. She'd seen newspaper accounts of other instances; she knew she wasn't the only one. The experts she read told her she wasn't to blame for being raped. Raped over and over again by frat boys. Six of them. Seven. More maybe. She couldn't say. She'd never be able to say for sure. She'd never told a soul. On the rumpled mattress of Jeb's twin bed upstairs in that giant warren of a house, the reek of booze, all that beer, the stench of her own vomit, and the musk of fluids she could still smell. The experts said she had had to forgive them, "forgive *herself*"—let go of the pain and anger and humiliation and paralyzing fear of them she still felt and get on with her life. Nearly two years after that night at the fraternity house she'd made herself go through with it with a guy she liked. His name was Todd. She'd gone stiff as a cadaver, her muscles locked. She had no control over her reaction, lost to it. Naked on her back on her bed, rigor mortis had set in. *What's the matter?* he asked. *Hey, are you okay? This is a little weird.* She'd stared over his shoulder at the ceiling, remembering. Mercifully, he'd pulled on his jeans and shirt and left. "I'll call you, all right?" he said, but, of course, he never had.

Jackie tucked her license back into her wallet and lit another cigarette. She felt the hollowness in her chest filling with the thumping pulse of nicotine coursing through her veins. Slowly her calm returned.

Before that night—the night of the Jif at the college where she'd gone that Wednesday with her girlfriends—Jackie had thought she might invest the college scholarship she'd earned in becoming an elementary schoolteacher as her mother had been before her. Before that night she had believed in words, and she had thought she might like to live to give the gift of reading to others. But now, Jackie knew, words weren't enough. They were extraordinarily inadequate at anything they meant to say. They didn't help. Words were only labels. *Gang-bang* was nothing to say. It was too easy. *Hate* was even easier; it didn't mean anything. *Forgiveness* was just a word unless you found the feeling for it first. Words did not give you anything inside yourself to grip onto—they were too smoothed free of pain—Jackie knew, Jackie had learned. Grief was *nothing* to *say*. And explanations for what had happened to her were worse than nothing, slants of blame, spinning guilt. The hurt— whatever that gash was whenever she thought of it, *now*, of what they did, what had been done, to *her*—they did not know her, or her mother, or where her father worked, her wish to be a teacher (to do that to another person, *How could you? How could they?*), the bile rising sour in her throat, the _____! which was the real rage and helplessness and wish for revenge—so strong, too strong—that the morning after, when she'd stumbled back to her dorm room and (somehow) gotten to the bus station, riding home alone scrunched against the window feeling indescribably weak, infinitesimally small, like a piece of shit (she had *felt* that, they had made her feel like that—a *cunt*, their word, a word she abhorred) she had gone home to her father. She could not think of another person to go to. Where else could she go? But on the bus ride home she knew too that her father would not take this to the law. Would he try to kill them? After having lost his wife, and now this, the following loss of his daughter? An act he could only find answer to with a shotgun blast to silence the frustration and anger pent up inside him—he had always hunted, guns were a natural part of his life. Or would it completely destroy him, knowing he was helpless to protect the women he loved more than he cared for his own life? And then what would happen to *him,* her father, who loved her and who couldn't protect them? What could she *do?* No matter what they'd done to her, she could not do that to *him,* her father who she loved as much as he loved her.

The feeling of what to do was beyond her, even in the racing and crazy thoughts, hungover, sick, so sore, torn between her legs, a constant throbbing reminder, thinking, imagining, *wishing,* beyond her. The truth could only be felt. And it was much too much to feel; there was no room inside herself to give vent to it; it would not come out. She imagined herself crazy—locked in the mental home she'd visited once with her class in junior high; herself as the woman who ran up to them laughing, red-tongued, and pulled down her pants to show them, girls and boys both. And so she'd done what she'd been able to imagine she could do to come to terms with what had happened to her—she could *not* go back to that school and face them: she'd run away.

Living with the inexplicable fact of that night in her life every day now for ten years was, for Jackie, like being a survivor of the aftermath of having been caught in any unpredictable, unfathomable disaster, a twister that comes swirling blackly out of the sky, or a hurricane, howling sixty-foot waves that rise whipped around the eye, catching a ship out to sea, the sudden irresponsible violence of a car crash which she hadn't glimpsed coming, sideswiped at any intersection, the impact and can-crumple of metal, shattering glass, riding it out to be left in the rocked silence with the blaring of a stuck horn. Except, a crash isn't evil.

The evilness filled her then and then the fast-flashed picture she could only imagine and could not stop imagining nor blink away: herself naked on a rumpled unmade bed, sweat and blood and cum-stained, while another boy climbed on top of her and jammed it in, hurting her with impunity—*fucking* her—the others standing around, talking, watching, waiting their turn, the overhead light was on—her head spinning, the sickness of it, too many beers, that tunnel blackness of having passed out, the sheer, slick walls of a well, no climbing up, and the faces at the top, *this* boy's face now in his lust, mouth parted, staring down, performing a fast pump with his hips, to make the other boys hoot and laugh and some other boy dangling his dick in her face. Started, it all started playing quarters for fun. She'd hooked up at the Jif with the sandy-haired boy they called Jeb, and they'd begun to dance. They'd had fun dancing, and she'd let go. Her roommates had gotten her to go out and she was having fun! Finally! After everything. All she'd been through. But she had a handsome boy and her friends had gone, bored, trying to tow her along. But Jeb promised he'd walk her home; that was how it was done. He'd promised. And then he and some of his brothers—he was nicknamed

Jeb, another the Walrus, another Dog Face, Webby, Muscle-head, Young Dave—had gotten out a card table in a back room, brought in a pitcher of beer from the keg. Jeb produced a shiny quarter. "Chug! Chug! Chug!" They bounced the damn thing in nearly every time. Everyone laughed. "Practice makes perfect!" The Walrus laughed and handed Jackie the glass again. "You drink!" Other boys came in to watch. She excused herself and weaved through the crowd, almost entirely boys now, the party winding down, toward the bathroom, sat with her face in her hands. "Home," she managed to get out when she came back, she didn't feel well, and Jeb grinned around the table.

"Choo-choo! Night Train!"

"Hey," he said walking her out into the hall, "why don't we go up to my room. You'll feel better if you lie down for a bit first." She nodded with relief and rested the heaviness of her head against his chest, thankful for his protection.

Jackie could not recall passing out in Jeb's room, no matter how she tried. She blurred in and out of the succession of faces, the same face, her mind aslur. She saw her own breasts jiggling white below her, and tried to cover them with her hands that were being held down, heard herself trying to be nice: *I'm sorry, but I have to go now.* Trying to be *polite,* saying, *Please,* even. And then, sitting at the Reef, she started to shake, felt it beginning from a deeper place than thinking inside her—a place she could usually stay out of the way of, busy at work at the dress shop or routinely walking Max in the mornings or sunning on the beach or having a margarita here at the Reef under Steve's watchful eye, but which could, if she wasn't careful, descend on her again like this without warning, like a plague—a black swarm of locusts devouring everything in their wake— everything about her gone dark as if she'd been locked inside a closet at night. But she'd been ready for it today.

She'd known it was coming—a day of reckoning. She was thirty. Her mother had died at forty-eight. *Her own life was sweeping away without her.* That single night in all her life's nights which had—as it turned out—controlled all the rest of her living since, managing her decisions; her existence on the planet up to this point which she could subtotal now sitting alone at the Reef before the golden glow of the window and the blue shining Gulf beyond. Why she'd withdrawn from school, left her father, left anyone she knew—anyone who had *known* of her and might have heard the boy's bragging rumors—*Man, we pulled a TRAIN on that black-haired chick Jackie last night*—had not fought them or pressed charges, had not gone straight to the police as she wished now she had done, as she would have done if she were not that twenty-year-old girl full of loss and hurt but the mature woman of thirty she found she was today, no matter what the consequences, but had run, *let them get away with it!* She had lied to her father and ridden a bus to Pensacola—a place she knew of only from a postcard she'd seen in her mother's scrapbook. It was the place where her mother and her father had met. He'd been in the service and she'd been teaching, her first job at the elementary school.

Jackie reached for her cigarettes, her fingers shaking like severed snakes. She had trouble aiming the flame. She set the pack down and leaned close to the table to tip another sip of her drink to steady herself.

The door opened, shining sunlight. A few flyers in leather jackets. Jackie glanced at her watch. Where had her afternoon gone? It was nearly 4:00. Time for her to go. She liked to sit at the Reef only in the early afternoons before the place packed up. She finished her second margarita and pulled her purse toward her. She stood too suddenly, feeling the tequila all at once.

"Jackie," Steve said and the men lined up at the bar all

swiveled about on their stools to look at her, to look her up and down. She was the only woman in the place.

"Where you going, gorgeous?" the golfer guy at the bar said. "It's your *birthday*. Look, why don't you lighten up a bit. Let me buy you another drink. Relax."

Steve stepped out from behind the bar to walk her to the door. Someone dropped a quarter in the old-time jukebox, and the record dropped, the speakers crackling, and then the music started up—a country tune, "Swingin'."

"Are you all right to drive?" Steve asked quietly, close to her ear beside her as he led her away.

"I'm fine," she said.

"Well," Steve said. They were standing beside the door. "Hey, would you like to go fishing on Sunday? Me and Sam are going to take the boat out."

Jackie stood close to him in the entranceway. "I have to work."

Steve grinned. "Talk to the manager!"

"Thanks for the drinks."

"Sure," he said. "Happy Birthday, Jackie. Drive safe now."

She nodded and pulled open the heavy door, feeling the men at the bar watching after her. She slipped out, the door banging closed behind her, shielding her. Jackie felt the relief. The late afternoon sunlight slanted into her eyes as she crunched across the gravel drive toward her car. Then she stopped. She wasn't as interested in going home as she had been in simply getting out of that bar before Steve got too busy to save her from one of the men who, invariably, would sidle up and sit down to talk. Jackie turned to the open beach she'd been watching through the tinted windows. At the edge of the parking lot, she bent and slipped out of her new sandals, carrying them in her left hand as she stepped onto the white sand that still held the heat of the day's sun. She was the only person on the beach. She walked in the direction of the National Preserve, the park where the dunes still rolled right down to the beach uninterrupted by the skyscraping bother of condominiums like her own.

A hot fall breeze gusted up behind her, pushing her faster down the beach, the wind wrapping her thin, summer dress tightly around her. She pulled it away from her, but the cloth grabbed violently at her body, whipping about her bottom and legs, shaping closely about her. From the direction of the parking lot, the layered smoke from a freshly lit cigarette caught up to her and ghosted past, going faster than she could run down the beach. She didn't dare to turn around. The man who'd been sitting at the bar in the Reef had followed her outside. She knew it. She could feel the sudden evilness of his presence in a shiver that raced up her spine, needling the hairs on her scalp.

She began to walk more quickly, stepping onto the hard-packed sand beside the water.

Jackie was walking fast now, nearly running. Then she broke into a run. But there was no place to go. No where to run. And suddenly she felt all the fear turn to fury, the rage boil into bravery, and she stopped and spun, turned to face him, dropping her bag and shoes, her fists doubled, screaming, *"Leave me alone!"* But the beach was deserted. There was no one behind her for as far as she could see. At the other end of the beach, a bright glow of green lights read THE REEF.

Back in her condo, Jackie fed Max his supper and turned on the TV. There were three messages on the answering machine. "Hey, Jackeline," her father said. He sounded tired, and she could imagine him in his washed blue Carbide cap, the half-moons of grease under his fingernails of his right hand as he lightly held onto the cord. "Just calling to wish you a happy birthday, honey. I'm home." The second was from one of the girls at The Limited who had a question about the fall stock they were to display at the store. Did Jackie want her to put the fall suits on the mannequins, or the black leather mini? The third was from Steve. In the background she could hear the jukebox and a waterfall of voices, a splash of laughter. "Jackie," Steve said loudly. "Just checking on you. If you feel like it, give me a call."

Jackie played his message back twice and then saved his voice. She walked into her bedroom and took off her dress. She reached for a hanger and then thought better of it, and tossed the dress in the hamper by the door. She reached around and unhooked her bra and, without letting herself glance at her breasts in the mirror—she'd had enough for one night—pulled on the sweatpants and T-shirt she'd walked in that morning. She twirled a scrunchy into her hair and bent to the sink and washed her face. She brushed her teeth. She was calm again. She felt perfectly straight; it was as if she hadn't even drunk those two drinks. She'd crumpled and then thrown the last pack of cigarettes she had into the trash can first thing when she'd walked through the door.

She was walking back out to the living room, where Max was already on the couch, thumping his tail for her to come watch TV, when the doorbell rang. It was nearly seven, and her shades were pulled, the door double-locked, the chain hooked across too. The long summer evenings were used up; the early dark had come. Winter lay in store. She felt the dread from her walk on the beach by the Reef return. Jackie crept barefooted into the hallway.

"Who is it?"

"It's me."

Jackie walked to the door and then she stepped up to the peephole. Steve stood outside, moths fluttering the halo of lamplight behind him.

Jackie unlocked the bolt; she took the chain off the door and pulled it open wide. Max's tail thwapped the walls in greeting.

"Steve," she said, "why aren't you at work?"

"I talked to the boss." He grinned sheepishly. Then shrugged. "We were slow. Diane can handle things. It's your birthday. I brought you this." He had a 7-Eleven bag in his hands. Jackie took the cold bag. "All the cakes were stale."

Jackie looked into the bag—fast-melting chocolate ice cream. She stepped aside holding the ice cream. "Come in."

Steve stepped inside, immediately filling the hall. Jackie didn't have many people in her home, and it felt odd to her to have to step around him as he leaned over to pat Max. "Nice place," he said.

In the kitchen she took down two bowls and set them on the counter. She didn't own an ice-cream scoop.

Steve was walking around her space, looking at her things. She watched him pick up the picture of her mother from the top of the TV.

"Is this your mom?" he asked. He looked up and Jackie nodded.

He looked carefully at the picture before he set it down again. "You guys could have been sisters."

Steve turned to her as she walked out of the kitchen with their bowls. She was struck again by the size of him, by the place he took up in her living room, by the way his very presence filled the hollow that was her home. He was looking at her, and she smiled, felt her face heat up. "Thank you for the ice cream."

He settled back onto the couch, his long legs thrust out before him. "You're welcome," he said. "It's been a strange evening. After you left the bar tonight, that guy in the pink shirt went out after you—the obnoxious one at the bar. I had a funny feeling about him. I followed him out into the parking lot and we both saw you walking on the beach toward the dunes. He didn't leave, just stood there on the edge of the lot smoking, watching you, until he saw me watching him. I stood there in the doorway with my arms crossed until he stubbed out his cigarette and climbed in his car. He was the kind of asshole that yells 'fuck you, buddy,' as he drives past. After he left, I had to go back inside. But I was still worried about you. I didn't like the idea of him loose out there. I even called here to see that you were okay. When I didn't hear from you, I called Diane to come in and take over for me."

Jackie watched Steve as he spoke. She looked down. Then she set the bowl of ice cream on the coffee table and stood.

She was standing in the dark of her bedroom with her back turned to the door. "Jackie?" Steve said from behind her in the dark. He sounded worried—or maybe it was his fear for her that she heard in his voice. He stepped into the room and reached out and touched her shoulder. "Hey, Jackie. I'm sorry. Did I say something wrong? I'm sorry, you know. I can go if you want."

Jackie turned to him then and pressed herself against his chest. She reached up to touch the tangle of his beard, found his lips with her fingertips and tiptoed up to kiss him, pressed the wet on her cheeks against him, between them. "Please," she said.

He undressed her slowly, and she lay back as he struggled off his T-shirt, hopped to get out of his boots. Lying naked on the bed, Jackie reached back and squeezed up two fistfuls of the sheets, thinking briefly of her first time with Jake, and braced for the pain that didn't come, felt Steve filling her body now as he had filled the hollowness of her home, large as he was, and it had been a long time. He was on top of her and she wrapped her arms around his wide back, she held onto him with her legs, rocked and rocked with him until he shuddered, saying her name, "Jackie," goose bumps rising all along his spine, and then, from inside that rocking, with him still inside her, she felt herself filling, and filling, until she thought she would burst, until she burst, and her body jumped and, on this day of her birth, came alive, born again by an act of love.

Clearing

In memory of Breece Pancake

All Pap ever wanted was a piece of land to call his own. He'd cuss and say that to me as we got up at 5:00 to go to the mines and grunt and say it again as we climbed in the truck to go home after our shift. And in the evenings, sitting out on the steps of our trailer drinking a cold one and watching off into the reds of a sunset, he'd look up at me and say, "If I had my druthers, I'd farm a little piece of land—yes I would." Sometimes he'd take me up to the clearing on top of the mountain, the evening sky opening up blue above us, and as we stood looking down at all the land that was out there just waiting to be had, he'd shake his head and try to laugh and say, "If I had the money that is." Now I had the money, insurance money.

Beside me Guy's gone to coughing again. I look up at him, his eyes squeezed into these tight white lines. I don't say anything though. We've been through it all before—what

Pap used to rhyme, "Black lung'll take what the cave-ins can't." I watch him spit a chunk of blood into his handkerchief and stuff it into his back pocket.

I'm carrying my silver lunch bucket with me and I tip my hard hat back with the weight of the light, try to tilt my head just right so that the coal dust won't run with the sweat into my eyes. Behind us the other miners are filing out of 18-D, stepping out onto the red-dog shale into the light, heading for the washhouse or getting into their trucks, standing straight up like men for the first time all day. Past them stands the tipple and all around the mess of dozer tracks and left stumps, the stinking smolder of the slag pile. I think how it wasn't two years ago that this hill used to be acres and acres of maple and virgin oak and the best damn deer hunting Pap and I ever came across. I bet myself that Myra will be at Jake's tonight. There's a logged oil filter laying in my way, stuck in the mud up to its neck. I give it a halfhearted kick with my steel-toed boot, which sends it no place. Don't budge it. Useless.

Guy is off and coughing again. "Hey," I say, "you all right?" and give him a good slap to help clear it. He shoves my arm away, says, "Damn it, Brunner!" But I don't pay him any mind. We're cousins but we've been more like brothers since Pap died. I stop to wait for him, one hand on my hip, dangling my pail against my leg. Guy goes stumbling right on by, working to hack up a whole lung it seems, his eyes jammed white against the pain.

"Hey, Guy," I say. "Guy!" I call. "My truck's over here, man." I shake my head. "Just goddamnit," I say, and then I start after him.

Jake's Place is hopping. I've got twenty-five dollars riding on the eight and I call it in the side pocket. I can feel Myra watching. She's standing up on a bench in back, looking over the crowd circled around the table. I've got a tough shot. The secret I know, though, is that I've already made it. I chalk my stick, Pap's stick, which is a famous one around here. Then I smile around the crowd, through the smoke. C.O. Burks ain't smiling though, got his thick arms crossed over his barrel chest—course it's his twenty-five bucks I'm about to make. I quit showboating and set my fingers to the felt. I smooth the stick long across the chalk-worn resting spot between my thumb and first finger and crouch to the ball, squinting an eye at the edge of the eight, call the side pocket again so no one will imagine it's a mistake, and put my stick through the cue ball firm. I stand up into all the talking and smile just like I seen Pap do a zillion times. I reach over and shake C.O.'s hand. "Maybe next time," I shrug to him, and fold his money away without bothering to count it.

I find Myra, wearing tight Levis and a yellow halter, at the bar talking to Brent Adams. I walk up beside her, edge between two stools, and call Jake to get me a Miller. Jake raises his red eyebrows to me, because everybody knows Myra's my girl. We started going out the month before Pap was killed, and she's been with me the whole time, through the funeral and all and ever since. Her daddy died in the mines too—when she was just a kid—and she's told me it's the memory of that black dust still caked under his nails at the viewing that's brought the tears back nights since. Lately, though, she says it's been the picture of my waxed and staring face laid out on that very same kitchen table at her mama's place that wakes her straight up, screaming. Last night I tried to soothe her. "Be patient," I said. "What is it they say? 'Good things come to those who wait?'" She pushed her hair back and looked me full in the face. "No," she said, "I think the way it goes is, 'The Lord helps those who help themselves,'" and she got up out of bed and grabbed her dress, backed out of the drive spraying gravel all over the place.

And now Myra keeps up talking to Brent Adams with her back to me. Brent smiles at that, and I think how maybe I'll just break his fucking neck, but instead I ignore her ignoring me and dig down in my pocket for quarters. I hear Brent telling her how he's just waiting for his uncle to get him on up at Werner Steel. Hear him say, "I should get the word any day now."

"Good for you," Myra says, sitting back and crossing her legs. "Good for you, Brent." She touches the red straw in her drink and shakes her head. "It sounds so *perfect*."

I stare at her brown hair and then I turn and leave her sitting there with him.

Guy's leaning up against the blue lights of the jukebox, and walking up, it startles me to realize just how much he's shrunk. His cheeks are all sucked up, and he's still losing weight—spitting up his guts in thick, mucoused chunks all day long. Guy nods toward the bar: "What she think she's doing?"

I shrug. "Hell if I know." I sure know all right, though. I tip up my beer and stick in my quarters and call up some Earl Scruggs and Waylon Jennings. I step back and glance over to the bar again. Brent's hand brushes Myra's thigh, and my arms pump tight. Guy shakes his head and then buries a cough in his fist.

"I just won twenty-five," I say to him. "You want to help me drink it up?" Guy grins. I lean my head toward the door, "Let's get the hell out of here then."

First thing we stop into the 7-Eleven and buy ourselves a case of Miller, then thunder my Chevy on up Route 10.

"You ever think about God?" Guy, his CAT DIESEL cap shoved way back on his forehead and his red hair curled up around the edges, is peeling at the label of the beer bottle between his legs.

"Sometimes," I say. When Pap died trapped down in that mine, I'd made up my mind about God—piss on him. But I don't say that. I wait for Guy to say something else. I watch him drink, his Adam's apple bobbing big. He kills it, rolls the empty under the springs of the seat, and reaches for another.

"If you think of it," I tell him, "get two."

As he pops mine, I think of Myra. "Werner Steel my ass," I say—screeching around the corner, fishtailing in the slick a bit—over the edge nothing but night blackness.

"*Christ*-a-mighty!" Guy yells, his feet wedged up against the dash, all scrunched up to save himself in case we crash. I look over at him, and then we both laugh right out loud about it.

I park the truck on a dirt boat ramp leading down to the Tug River. The water's oily-smooth and even blacker than the night. The dead-fish smell hangs over the body of a carp washed up on the bank. Down aways an old steel bridge spans the river, rattling like thunder with the string of headlights crossing it. When I was a kid, me and Pap would sit around a fire like this, frying up the catfish we'd caught. If he was drinking, he'd tell me about Ma. She'd always wanted to be a movie star. Then, finally, she'd just up and run off—left us for some long-haul trucker from Logan. "Impatient, I guess," is what Pap shrugged and said, slugging a shot down hard behind it.

I'm feeling my beers. Guy's laying on his back searching the summer stars himself. The water laps up against the rocks. Guy sits up quick, coughing. He spits. Spits again. He wipes across his mouth with the back of his bare hand. "Seriously, though," he says. "I'm thinking I might give my life to Jesus." He looks at me. I sip my beer and watch his eyes, his thick eyebrows scrunched down, heavy with it. I look away from him out over the water as the dark growling hulk of a tug shoves a barge of coal past us, slapping out waves against the shore.

The next day's Saturday, and I get up about noon to wash my truck. I'm outside next to my trailer when Myra crunches back up the gravel drive in her mother's Pontiac station wagon, Coke-bottle green with wood paneling. She's wearing cutoffs over a blue one-piece, her brown hair pulled back away from her face, no makeup. Her mama owned the only real beauty parlor in town, but Myra didn't want to be a beauty operator. She kept hinting that after we got married she might like to go back to school and learn to teach. In her handbag I'd found the *Pennysaver* with the blue circles around all the farms for sale, and when we sat together on the red vinyl couch in her mama's place, she'd close her green eyes and flip through one of the magazines, point at some shiny page, then open them again and lean forward to squint at where she'd landed us. "Well, how'd you like to live in Hawaii?" she'd say, smiling brightly. I turn the hose hard against my windshield but still hear her flip-flops flapping up behind me. I let off the pressure on the handle and face her.

"You have a time with Brent Adams?"

She doesn't say anything. Then she sighs. She shakes her head and then she just laughs, dropping it. "No, not particularly," she says, "but that's not the point, is it?"

"It *isn't?*" I look at her. And then I turn back to my truck, counting down from fifteen to bring me back from boiling as I reach a hand down into the bucket of soap, pull out the sponge, squat down and start in on the bug-spattered chrome. I give a few quick swipes to my rebel-flag license plate on front. "Look, Brunner," she starts. "Would you please just listen to me for a second?" She steps up and squats down behind me, pressing against my back, and reaches around me like that for a hug. "All I'm trying to say is. . . ." But I don't pay her any mind. I concentrate on a yellow jacket that has managed to get himself squashed under the bolt, just his stinger sticking out. She is hugging me from behind and then her hand wanders down and she starts to rub me through my jeans, teasing me. "Oh, Brun-ner," she says.

"What's the matter," I start, my voice going up. "Brent didn't give you enough?" I wanted to hurt her like she could hurt me.

"You know what, Brunner?" she says, getting up on her tiptoes. "You're a goddamn idiot." She bends back down and kisses the top of my head.

Late that night it's me who wakes with a start and can't get back to sleep. I sit looking out the bedroom window down into the black hollow. Ever since his funeral I've been telling myself that Pap would want me to leave—would be righteously pissed if he knew I was down in the mines again after what happened to him—would *insist*. "Goddamnit, son!" I hear him holler. "Shit or get off the pot!" And I smile because it rings true. Once I'd gone so far as to haggle over the price on two hundred acres in Kentucky, tobacco land. But I can't seem to go any further. I think how everything I've ever really known is here. I wonder, would Pap under-stand? I conjure up his face again, pores black with years of coal dust as he pressed that sweating beer can against his lips, his eyes searching far away—maybe thinking about my ma running off or about some little piece of land he might've farmed—focused on beating that setting sun back up by 5:00 to be on time at the mines the next morning.

The moonlight ripples across the curtains in the fan air. Myra's asleep on top of the sheets, turned on her side, one breast pressed full against her arm, real white. I kiss her lightly, feel her even breath on mine—breathing back into me—that something about her I can't ever seem to name. There isn't a word I can think of exactly as close as I need it to be. I walk out of the room into the kitchen and grab a beer, the refrigerator light cutting me off white at the knees.

Outside, on the front steps, I sit down and pop the top. High up I catch the winking red-dot lights of a plane. It is quiet and cool, surrounded by the dark hills. I tell myself, for the millionth time, it really isn't difficult—I've got the jack—I can leave, anytime. The screen door unlatches behind me and I turn to see Myra standing in one of my old T-shirts.

She sits down beside me, and I hand her the beer. "You make it a habit of sitting outside naked?" she asks, smiling, tucking her hair back behind her ear. Her thigh is warm and smooth along the length of mine. She takes a sip and hands me back the can.

"So, you really want to get married?" I say.

She's quiet. I feel her watching me.

"You know I couldn't make this kind of money no where else."

"It's not about the money," she says.

"Well, it wouldn't be easy either." I turn to see my eyes searching back at me through hers. "I mean starting all over, everything new, not knowing nobody..."

"...leaving your pap behind." She puts her arm through mine. "Please don't go back down in those mines and make me have to leave you for someone like that Brent Adams, Brunner."

I pull away, sit up straight, and arch against the tightness in my lower back—we have begun again and gone around and stopped in exactly the same sticking place we always have.

Myra tickles her fingernails down my spine. "Come on back to bed," she says. An owl hoo-hoots and glides. I let out a sigh, shake my head. I'd be tired at work in the morning.

Every night for the next two weeks, Guy sneaks off to some revival at the Antioch Baptist Church. I don't even try to go to Jake's after my shift—just clean up in the washhouse and head straight home to sit in front of the television by myself. Between shows, I think of trying to call Myra at her mama's house, but the closest I get is lifting the receiver up off its cradle and holding it against my chest. The night I finally break down and call, it's her mama who picks it up from downstairs in the shop. *"Jenete's,"* she says with the script of it still in her voice, though it is ten o'clock and I know that she's been working since eight that morning. I imagine the smell of a whole day of permanents singed out behind her.

"This is Brunner, Jean," I say to her. "Is Myra there?"

It hangs like that between us for a moment, loaded up. Then she says, starting slow, "No, Brunner. I'm sorry, I'm afraid she's not."

"Oh?" I say, and then I say, "Well, okay. Will you just tell her I called then?" And before she has a chance to sympathize or anything, *I* cut in on myself, saying, "Well, I appreciate it." and hang up the phone just that quick. Then I sit on the couch for the longest time, hoping—from all I've heard going around town about the two of them—that Brent Adams knows just what a lucky man he is to have her.

The next morning, Guy's carrying one of those little green Gideon Bibles with him down in the mine and every chance he gets he's reading in it, his lips moving with the words in his lamplight. I ask him if he's handling snakes yet, but he's gone too good to smack me back. On Friday he tries to get me to go with him, having a fish fry or something out at the church, puts his hand on my shoulder and says that Jesus can save me too, but I shrug him off. "Don't touch me," I tell him and I feel my fists knot up. It seems he's coughing up less blood, and he says, "You know, Brunner, the Lord works in strange ways." I say, "Fuck that," and he won't talk to me for the rest of the day.

That very Sunday, Guy gets baptized in the Tug River, gets reborn, and announces he isn't going down into the mines anymore. He shows up in his Jeep, his hair still wet, dressed in his sky-blue suit, white shirt and wide black tie, black shoes and white socks. He gives me a little silver cross on a chain. It says "JESUS SAVES" so that the middle "S" going across in JESUS is in the beginning of SAVES going down.

"This is what I been wearing down in the mines for ten years," he says, standing just outside the screen door of my trailer. I take the cross and dangle it from its chain. If I think about it, I can see it around his neck all the time in the washhouse. Guy has this smile on his face like he's about to bust wide open at the seams.

"Well, how about a beer to celebrate?" I say.

He frowns. "Can't," he says. "I give up drinking."

Monday morning it feels strange to sit in the waiting room and ride the cage down into 18-D without Guy. It was the same the first couple of weeks after Pap died, like I'd forgot something, left it behind. Everybody's heard about Guy and comes up to ask me about him. I just shrug and tell them he's been saved. I don't have anything else to say. I climb into the mantrip and feel the rough wood seat through the thick canvas skin of my pants. The bells ring twice, and we all duck down as the electric motors rumble us deeper into the mountain, our headlamps bobbing ghosts into the darkness.

Mitch sticks me with Brent Adams. I take Mitch by the arm and tell him I don't think I ought to work with Adams. He tells me he doesn't give a good goddamn in hell who I think I *ought* to work with. He's pissed because Guy's my cousin and he just up and quit like that. There're plenty of men out there to hire, but Guy's a timberman who knows his stuff.

I crawl back up the hole and through the trapdoor, pick up a cap piece to use as a kind of cane. It makes moving bent over a lot easier, scuttling along like some three-legged crab, and I don't bother to wait and see if Brent can keep up.

At the pile of logs, I pull out a piece of wire and tie it around one of the props. I put my weight into the wire and drag the prop behind me back to the trapdoor. It's heavy and I'm already starting to sweat. I squeeze past Brent on my way back to the logs—just making it down now for his first trip. After we get all the logs piled up by the trapdoor, I hold onto my hat and go through. The wind grabs at me. When Brent gets through and shuts the door, it booms down the shaft and the wind quits. I take out my Redman and pinch out three fingers but I don't offer Brent any— sweet like that. Then I start to load the props on an old, rusted, three-wheeled cart. We push and pull it to a caved-in section where we can stand straight up. The roof here has come down in sharp angles to about fifteen feet, rocks jabbing out in ragged steps. We are close to the big fan, and I feel my sweat go cold. Every time I see a cave-in, I get this flash of me picking out that Cadillac-model coffin I buried Pap in. As I reach up to measure off the height of the roof with a long stick, I imagine that undertaker again—measuring this custom one off to fit my own lanky legs. I need a prop.

Brent's squatting down with his arms on his knees. I just look at him.

"Little help?" I say.

He grunts, gets up and walks over to the prop and holds while I saw. I take the prop and put it in place, stick a shim in each side, tap them up tight with the flat of my axe. Then I measure off for the next prop. I turn and Brent is squatting down again. Jesus Saves, I think. I could've punched Guy good.

After work, I head straight for the washhouse to get cleaned up to go home. I put on my jeans and pull out my comb, am turning toward the bank of mirrors when I hear Brent's voice echo from the showers. *"Hell no,"* he says, "no. I ain't leaving—leaving," I hear. "I don't even *have* an uncle." There is a steaming silence and then they explode together over it, laughing, hooting and howling, barking big. "But Lordy," he yells over the roar, "was she ever *primed* for it!"—setting them off again.

I stand in front of the mirrors with the comb in my hand, watching myself drain white and then blast off red. I forget my hair, tuck the comb in my back pocket, and step past the green benches, walk past the clothes dripping from baskets, over to the entrance of the showers, and stand there looking in. Water patters against the concrete. Brent has his back turned and is soaping off his face in the spray, his big hairy butt all splotched pink from the hot water. He turns with his eyes closed, and the water trickles over his nose, matting his hair, glistening over his belly and off his dick.

Everyone goes quiet, watching me. Just the splatter of water. Brent opens his eyes and smiles. "Well," he says, "if it ain't the Timberman." I just stare at him. He turns off the water, wipes at his face, and tries to step out of the shower room past me, but I block his way. He stops. I take a fast swing and catch him good in the mouth. I tackle him back hard into the wall. He's punching my kidneys. We crash to the floor and I punch at his face. I have him on his back, but he's slippery. He catches me just above the eye. Then in the stomach. I land one. He tips me off. Water splashes. I try to choke him, and he bites my wrist hard. He hits me again in the eye. Then someone pulls him off. I scramble up but there are men between us now. "You crazy motherfucker!" Brent yells. His mouth is bleeding. My left eye feels closed shut. I shove their arms away and go straight back to my bucket and grab the rest of my clothes, wiping his blood from my bared knuckles that I know has mingled with my own—my heart still beating too hard to let me believe I have solved anything. I drive back to my trailer in wet jeans.

In my own kitchen I crack the seal on a bottle of Jim Beam and feel around for a glass in the old coffee grounds and plates soaking in the sink. The phone rings, but I just watch it. I can't imagine anyone I could possibly want to talk to right now. Giving up on a glass, I grab the bottle by the neck and bang out the door.

I have to put my truck in four-wheel drive to pull up the mountain—powering over rocks, gearing into low. My truck takes it like a tank. I keep the bottle squeezed tight between my legs. The cross Guy gave me hangs on the rearview mirror alongside the red and white tassel from my high school graduation, and it lurches with the ruts in the road. Molly Hatchet's cranked up on the stereo.

In the clearing at the top of the mountain the sun is blood-orange, and I'm considering a drunk. In the side view the gash above my left eye is already purple-deep and tinted yellow—*my eyes*, but it's Brent's voice I hear echoing up from deep inside. *I don't even have an uncle.* "Jesus Christ,"

I say. I stomp the emergency break, reach for the keys and cut the engine, shove out the truck door into the clearing.

The pine trees up here, which I remember as freshly sprouted, have already been weathered grey and stripped by the winds. I watch as the eastern sky darkens into a royal blue, flashing stars and a quarter moon, the sun still glowing over the mountains in the west. Down below me are the scars of the mines—much deeper than they look from here—fire roads stitched back and forth across the mountain. A cover of fog hangs close to the river and winds off into the low hollows. I close my eyes to it, feeling the brace of the wind on my face, and take in a long deep breath of the clean air to calm myself.

Up here Pap'd always said he could get clean air and clear out his lungs as well as his head. He'd always said up here a man could open up his eyes and see for a long time. And opening up my eyes now and looking down over the mines and into these hollows, I can see what he must must have seen for himself. I can see *my* whole life, everything I've ever done and about every place I've ever been. I can even see across the Tug River into Kentucky, but then the mountains stand up and block my view, and I can't see any further. *If I had my druthers. . . .* And just like that I know something else, what my mama must have known for sure, too, before she'd hiked herself up into the cab of that truck with that fellow from Logan. I reach for the bottle in my back pocket—unscrew the cap—think again. I screw it back, stow it.

I stand there in the clearing for a long time after that before I start back toward my truck. As I turn, I'm jumped by the snort of a buck, his head up, startled himself, nostrils flaring, the wind behind us both, before he slides into shadows so pure I can't swear I really saw him. Then I hear

Pap's murmured voice again, gusted away before I have a chance to understand. The hairs prickle up on the back of my neck and I spin to catch him—the royal sky, the pine, the quarter moon. Me, by myself, standing underneath them. I look up as the cross Guy gave me angles the last of the sunset and flashes it like a wet spot of blood, and I climb in my truck and go to her.

The Archaeological Society of Dancing Rabbit Creek

For Sarah

I

The day we discovered them, I had Hank Simmes in the chair, a few other farmers lined up along the wall curtained behind newspapers waiting their turn at a trim, when the bell jumped jangling and Bobby Lee stumbled in. The farmers glanced up at him standing there panting with his hand on the knob. Some folks in Dancing Rabbit Creek think Bobby Lee a crank because he has chosen to live out his life tree-hugging onto the past. Bobby Lee does not believe in electricity or automobiles either. Telephones, for him, are out of the question. His pale eyes cast around, caught mine. His went wide. "The Fletchers are planing Little Big Mound!" I looked at him and then reached for the hand mirror and showed Hank the bald back of his head. "This one's on me Hank," I said, unpinned him and flapped the cape. I flipped the CLOSED sign over and left him and the others sitting agape, grabbed my safari hat and canvas sack and headed for the back door still wearing my blue barber's smock, looking like a surgeon rousted out of the hospital on an emergency call. Bobby Lee had already rung out the front door ahead of me at a run to Revere on the alarm.

My old Toyota wouldn't go fast enough. I still had one of those blue lights left on top from my younger days when I used to perform my civic duty as a volunteer fireman, and I flipped it on and raced to the site. What I found when I arrived was a stretch of uninterupted blue where once the rise of Little Big Mound had filled the sky. The Choctow used to live here, occupied this Delta county from Greenville on the wide Mississippi west to Greenwood on the muddy Yazoo, north from the town of Rome forty-nine miles south to the X-marks-the-spot where the Yellow crosses the Dog—this stretch of land which we'd "bought" from them in 1830 with the Treaty of Dancing Rabbit Creek. For ten thousand years before the Choctow—on this same lowland which a geologist will tell you once laid flat as the floor of the Gulf—this place was home to the Mound Builders, the secret of their lives left at rest for us in these humps of earth like Little Big Mound that form a constellation of clues across our flat country. Now where the star of Little Big Mound had been an earthmover hunkered in its space, the diesel smoldering. Deere tractors stood by ready to disk in behind it and whip the wasted acerage into the shape of four acres more of cotton or soy—something to make on the moment without a care or consideration for the long-term investment humped up here in our past.

V.Z. Fletcher and some other boys clumped crowded in a bunch. I screeched to a halt, jumped out of my truck, and donned my safari hat. They all turned to look at me and then looked back as I hustled to the edge. The mound had been leveled, revealing a gaping hole. The miracle I saw, besides the sheer miracle of time, of a pocket of protection against the slow seep of water, the disintegrating touch of air, was that after the blade scraped over, the driver, on his next pass, had had the good sense to look down. Lying there was a pair of skeletons, perfectly preserved. They were as tiny as children, though obviously full-grown in the knobs of their knees, their ribs and femors and forearms aged root brown, their ankles and elbows and heads stained crimson by the gumbo clay that'd encased them for ten thousand years. But what held us staring, transfixed, was that they were lying there holding hands.

V.Z. was not too pleased to see me. He had a schedule to keep if he wanted to get crops into the ground that season; there was money to be made. He's not a bad man, just a farmer trying to make a living, and busy. He has the present to worry about and has no time for the past. If he could've quickly buried these folks back again before I'd seen them, he would've avoided days, maybe weeks, months, even years of red tape. Now the whole field could well be designated a landmark. Protected by the federal government, which, the plain fact of the matter is, none of us down here can stand. At the very least, once we'd alerted him to the discovery, it would bring in Dr. Steven Brain and his slow-digging team from the university. "Well, you've seen them," he growled and waved for the driver to continue, "I've got seeds to plant." I looked at him. Without a word, I pocketed my canvas sack, and climbed down into the pit. I nestled between them, careful not to disturb anything, took off my hard hat and clasped it over my heart. "Oh, come on, Sam!" he said. I've been the barber in Dancing Rabbit Creek for over forty years and have been cutting his hair since he was a kid. He had a Pleiades of moles over his left ear in exactly the same place his granddaddy and his daddy did, as his son has. I heard a cavalry of cars pull up. The rush of a truck.

"Jesus H. Christ," V.Z. said, disgusted, and turned away, kicking earth. I grinned up at Bobby Lee and George Chatham and Jack Lancaster and Willie Huckabee, who'd run up only to stop, staring down—their mouths Ohed up as round as if they'd glimpsed me in my opened grave.

II

Back in my shop that night, the five of us sat pondering what we'd found. We call ourselves the Archaeological Society of Dancing Rabbit Creek and our motto is: *Uncovering History Not Yet Written*. Except for me, who can flip the CLOSED sign over in the window of my barbershop any time I like, we're all full-time retired, four old widowers and Bobby Lee who never married. The upshot of all this loneliness is, of course, that we old duffers don't have much else better to do when we're not busy burying someone but to dig stuff up. The irony is never far off for us that soon enough we will be history ourselves.

Jack Lancaster was shaking his head. He'd taught algebra at the Academy for over thirty years, and you could tell how the afternoon had added up for him. "Did you *see* them?" he said. We nodded sympathetically. Jack's Betty had succumbed to pneumonia only that past winter. He is a tall, quiet, dignified man, and one of the toughest things I ever had to face up to in my life was watching him break down and cry. George Chatham had a bottle of Comfort. As the president of Trust Bank, he'd been a good listener always able to make you believe your problems or plans for applying for a loan were his own. He nodded at Jack's shaking his head and took a healthy slug before passing the bottle on. The fact of the matter is, George's wife, Isabel, was one of the sweetest women I had ever met, but she loved her More cigarettes. Now George got up and walked out of my shop if anyone so much as lit up and a time too when he was the guy stinking the place up with a fat cigar. Willie Huckabee was next in line. He'd been a retail buyer for Lewis's Department Store and had always been able to work a deal, but his wife, Honey, had ended her days in a daze with Alzheimer's and left him at his wits end. Me and Bobby Lee were the only two official members of the society back then and we'd be driving home late from a dig to see her waiting at the edge of the bayou in nothing but a pale pink negligee, Willie down on one knee begging her to come home. In her head she was a little girl again and insisted her daddy was coming in the wagon to pick her up—her daddy dead and been dead twenty years if he'd been dead a day. It was sure a sad thing to see. She wound up in the state hospital where Willie went to sit with her everyday from 1:00 till 3:00, though he said she didn't recognize him or any of their boys or even remember her own fun-to-say Honey Huckabee name. The Comfort came to me. I poured a dollop in my coffee cup with the logo: *Even Old Archaeologists Can Dust It Off and Get It Up*. My own wife, Allenade, died of the cancer four years ago on the first day of spring. It began in her ovaries, ate up our chance at children, then after the sure cure of forty-two years the cancer struck again in her spleen to ravage the rest of her past skinny, suck away her cheeks, the fullness of her smile. The boys helped me shoulder her coffin out of the church and slide it into the hearse, as I was to end up helping each of them. I buried her in Whispering Pines Cemetery at the edge of town.

I held the bottle out to Jack who was still shaking his head. "I mean did you *see* them?" he said.

Of course, I knew exactly what Jack meant. To date, as a society, we'd managed to dig up a few arrowheads that we'd donated to the local museum. Mostly, though, we'd dug up pots with holes and pans without handles, an old busted musket and a bucket full of smooshed bullets from the war, a rust-eaten wheelbarrow, the complete bleached skull of a cow, modern-day hoes. We'd uncovered mule harnesses and bricks, spark plugs and blue-green milk of magnesia bottles, a jar full of quarters and pennies galore, a silver dollar stamped with the homely face of Susan B. Anthony, and even a pearl-inlaid gutta-percha comb. Once, we'd discovered a single Adam's rib, which we wrapped up and rushed with my blue siren flashing to Dr. Brain, who looked it over, rubbing his chin, but said that most likely it was from a field-dressed deer. But we'd never uncovered anything as significant as a Dalton Point or a Choctow ceremonial bowl before, much less two skeletons so perfectly preserved, and even if we had, I don't think we could've ever imagined a man and woman buried for all those years together still holding hands. It was, without a doubt, the most crucial find the Archaeological Society of Dancing Rabbit Creek had ever made.

III

The next morning, on my way back to the site at Little Big Mound, I stopped by Whispering Pines. I drove the labyrinth of gravel roads back to the chinaberry I'd planted to shade my wife's spot, and climbed out of my truck.

A double-wide granite stone marks Allenade's place in this earth. A mature woman when she died, after the scare of having had cancer the first time, my wife had had quite a while to consider the actualities of dying. And so, on our way home from the hospital the afternoon the cancer was diagnosed the second time—the doctors in Memphis had tagged her with a less-than-six-weeks expectancy to live— she'd had me take a right instead of a left when we turned off Highway 46 and drive straight here, so she could flag off the plot she'd had her eye on all that long while since. Then she'd had me ride her over to Pritchard's Funeral Home to look at coffins. Allenade strode straight into the front show-room and began to shop around. I coughed into my fist, but she was looking seriously at the prospects—opening lids and closing them, knuckling the mahogany to see whether it was simply veneer. There were brochures for the coffins, too, fanned out on a doily on top of a little desk by the door, slicked up in blues and reds and greens. They had "Deluxe" models, "Economy" even.

"Frank!" Allenade called out into the church-like quiet, startling me so badly that I jumped, dropping the car keys. "Do you want to make a sale or not?" Frank Pritchard stepped out of the back looking long-faced trying to smile, rubbing his hands together as if he'd found a fire. Allenade settled on a middle-of-the-road model with a cloud-soft pink satin lining. She clasped her own palms together and asked Frank if he could leave us alone a moment with her decision, and when he slid the doors closed behind him, she winked at me, pulled up a chair, and climbed in. "All right, I'm ready. Shut the top," she said.

"Allenade. . . ."

"Humor me, Sam. I might as well be comfortable, don't you think?"

I glanced back at the door and stepped up, went so far as to lay my hand on the edge of the lid, but I couldn't make myself do it. "Dear," I began again.

"No need to be a scaredy-cat, Sam," she said and reached up for herself and thunked the lid down tight. I waited for her to knock or push it open. A minute ticked by, as eternally long as a minute can be. On the other side of the door, Frank cleared his throat; I could hear him tapping his foot to the time of the ticks of the grandfather clock in the entranceway.

"Allenade," I hissed, *"Allenade!"* then I panicked and threw open the lid, afraid she'd suffocated and I'd stood by like an idiot. In fact, she was dead asleep. Her mouth gaped open the way it sometimes did when she was especially tired.

When Frank came back in, she told him that model would be fine. She told me then how she'd been saving a quarter or a nickel, pennies or a dime for all those years since. I winced when she wrote Frank out a check from her own account.

She made up a list for the rest:

She requested lilies and wrote out R.S.V.P. invitations. She ordered the cold cuts and planned the reception herself, to be held at the Masonic Lodge two doors down from the funeral home. She wanted Reverend Roberts, long past senile, and not Reverend Smith, who didn't care a fig whether or not women wore hats to church, to say the final words over her. When I hinted that Reverend Roberts might not remember who he was saying the eulogy for, she only shrugged. "It'll be on the tombstone to read if he forgets." It was that tombstone which she cared most about and which she spent days picking out, choosing it as carefully as she would that single hat she was going to allow herself to pack on a month-long trip full of four possibilities for Sundays— a double-wide white granite marker joined at the curve of two hearts to cover us both.

It's true, all of her preparations to die had seemed odd to me then, but then I had years left to live. I can see now that Allenade dealt with her imminent death the way she'd always handled our life together and the only way she knew how. She met it as graciously as if death were any distant relative she'd only heard stories of but whom she'd gotten a card from asking if he might drop by for a visit as long as he was in the neighborhood. She would put her house in order, pat her hair in the hall mirror, and greet him at the door with a lipsticked smile. I remember we were sitting quietly side by side in our wingback chairs one night when Allenade looked up from the book she was reading to tip down her glasses and look blue-eyed over them at me. Then she closed the book and came to sit on my lap with me in my chair. She traced her finger along my chin and said, "I imagine you're going to go on living for awhile yet, Sam. You got good genes. Your great grandmama McGahey lived to be ninety-three." Then she gave me that shameless smile which we both knew what it meant—a bold wink which ladies did not do back then. "But I'll be waiting on you when you're ready to come to bed, dear." Next came the afternoon she'd fainted in front of her classroom as she was diagramming a complex sentence, and they'd moved her into the hospital full-time. From that night on until the day she died and I had to bury her alone in our couple's grave, I slept in the railed twin by her side.

It wasn't until the Christmas after I'd buried her that I found Allenade hadn't only picked out the double-wide tombstone to cover us both and taken care of all her own arrangements, she'd had the foresight to order a coffin for me as well. It came special delivery by truck straight out of the catalogue from that company in Memphis. She chose a matching middle-of-the-road model just like hers, but with a blue silk lining instead of pink. I just stood looking at the two fellows who delivered it, holding each end as if it were a couch from J.C. Penny. I had them put it in the shed, where it's sat on sawhorses ever since.

The boys thought *that* was a little more than just strange—that maybe she'd overstepped some inviolable boundary by planning my death, too—but I understood Allenade's sending on that coffin to me for what it was. Allenade meant it exactly as she had when, in living our day-to-day life together, she'd laid out my shirt and tie each morning, matched up my socks for me the way she would for any journey, whether preparing me for a day of cutting hair or for the time we drove three days to visit her family in Kentucky or for our honeymoon trip to Ruby Falls. The fact of the matter is that coffin was an absolutely selfless gesture of love.

When I finally arrived at the site, I found that Dr. Brain and his team from the university had already arrived. Vaiden Hamilton, the sheriff, was also there, his deputies posting off the dig.

"Morning Sam," Sheriff Vaiden said. "What have you old boys dug up this time?"

I shrugged, still feeling smug about the job that we as a society had done in preserving the find of the two skeletons. "I imagine what we've got here is a pair from the Paleolithic age. I'd say what we've got here, Sheriff, is quite a find."

Sheriff Vaiden stuck out his bottom lip and thumbed back over his shoulder at the gnat-thick swarm of reporters hovering about the scene. "I'll say."

News of our discovery had gone out over the wire after George Chatham had alerted Dr. Brain and his team at the university that what the Archaeological Society of Dancing Rabbit Creek had found this time might have more importance than any old rib from a field-dressed deer, and the announcement of a couple who had been together for ten thousand years had created the kind of sensation linked to the past that only an earthquake's shaking or a volcano's raging off in the present usually can. Dr. Brain himself was standing at the edge of the pit with his thumbs hooked under his lapels, a yellow bow tie reflecting as brightly as a buttercup under his chin, looking around looking pleased. TV lights bathed the skeletons bright. From where I stood, the two of them looked awfully naked. Exposed. The team from the university had just begun their excavation, and the dirt still left covering the skeletons made them seem as if they were trying to cover up, hoping to bury themselves back again from the prying eyes that sought to paw them up. Suddenly I felt their embarrassment in my own old bones. Beside me, Jack Lancaster said, "Damn," red-faced, and turned away.

IV

Late that afternoon I flipped the CLOSED sign over in the window of my shop and pulled down the blinds to hold an emergency meeting of the Society. Airing on the TV high in the corner was a talk show entitled: "Eternal Love: All You Ever Wanted to Know about Keeping Your Mate Forever." The big-toothed blonde woman gripping the microphone called our skeletons "the love-find of the century—a couple who'd stuck together for ten thousand years." The red-headed love therapist in the chair with the short-short leopard-print skirt nodded big. They had film footage of Dr. Brain down in the pit beside them, looking like a kind of therapist himself, touching their joined hands at the wrists as if he were taking the pulse of their relationship. The camera moved in for a close-up of their hands joined, worn by the weather and stained by clay but not torn asunder by worms or dirt or rain, joined still, a kind of miracle, through all those thousands of years. A computer-imposed image showed a man and a woman, squat and dark. "This could be any man," the love therapist was saying. "Any woman." Bobby Lee was ogling the televison, his face bathed a kind of radioactive green. Her skirt was awfully short, I felt that in my own heart. Next, three modern-day couples came on to talk about love. One couple had been married fifty years, another twenty-five years, the third were newlyweds. They all held hands while they talked. They didn't bother to have on as guests any lonely old widowers like us, men and women, too, who might've had something vital to say about what it meant to try to live on alone. George grabbed the clicker and flicked them off.

After a long silence, Willie Huckabee asked what we were going to do. We were, he said, *responsible*.

We opened the floor, and George Chatham immediately suggested we sue. We all thought that was a pretty good idea and talked about it for a long while, but none of us could figure out exactly *who* to sue. Bobby Lee, playing it straight, wondered if all the commotion wouldn't simply die away. But it was Jack Lancaster who suggested we simply bury them back again.

"You mean *steal* them?" George Chatham spluttered.

"I mean put them back where they belong. Think about your Isabel, George," Jack said. "Your Honey, Willie. Your Allenade, Sam. Think about the past Bobby Lee. Me? I'm thinking about my Betty."

It was the most I'd ever heard Jack say at a stretch; we didn't even need to put it to a show of hands. Willie put the risk we'd be taking in its proper perspective. He slapped George on the back and laughed, broke up cackling, hacking near to give up a lung. "Hell, what are they going to do if they catch us, George, sentence us to *life?*"

We decided to do the job that night.

We dressed in those remnants of our World War Two uniforms that we could still fit into—mostly caps and boots, though Jack rediscovered the perfect fit of a shirt which when issued had been two sizes too large—and blackened our faces with soot from George's barbecue grill. Then we piled into my truck and drove to the site.

The publicity the couple had gotten had forced Sheriff Vaiden to leave one deputy on all night. No one was really concerned that someone was going to steal the skeletons whole, but rather that with all the publicity they'd gotten, someone might damage them or try to swipe a bone, maybe that extra rib or one of the fingers which had been holding on for so long as a kind of good luck charm to help them go the distance in their own marriage. The deputy left to do the job was a boy by the name of Jed Daniels. Jed was a monster. He'd been a tackle on the football team at state and had graduated with a degree in criminal justice and two bum knees. I'd been cutting his scrub of red hair for him since he was a boy. The fact about him I knew was that he suffered from narcolepsy and without fail would doze off right in my chair. When Jed Daniels slept, he went out like a bear in hibernation, deep—but like any bear, Sheriff Vaiden knew too, the sheer size of him would do to keep intruders away. But I knew him well, and all we had to do, I told the boys, was wait. We had just settled down to some double-fudge pecan brownies Willie had baked and brought in a tin when Jack elbowed me. Jed had propped himself against a tree; his chin was resting against his chest. We sprung into action.

Our plan was simple: dig the skeletons up and get them out of there, quick. We stumbled down into the pit grabbing and slapping and tugging at each other's uniforms for balance. Bobby Lee stayed poised at the foxhole edge to keep an eye on Jed while George flapped the tarp out like a picnic blanket beside them, and me and Willie and Jack, still in our World War Two mode, went at them in our best-remembered imitation of asses and elbows, now more like an ache of backs and creak of joints. We took a lot of dirt with them, trying not to break them apart. Dr. Brain and his team had been at them all day with scalpel-sized shovels and brushes. Theirs had been the careful, painstaking archaeologists' job; we were simply acting as old men on a mission of love. A shinbone fell off, and George grunted down to pick it up, looked around, then shrugged and tossed it on the canvas. We flapped the edges over and pitched in, heave-hoing to lug them up the side, wiping sweat with every other step. Bobby Lee gave the all-clear Boy Scout's whippoorwill whistle, and we crested the edge. We huffed and puffed off into the shadows and stumbled through the woods to where we'd parked, two of us on each side acting as pallbearers, and settled the skeletons gently down into the blue silk lining of my coffin, which we'd stopped by the house on our way there to pick up. We closed the lid, lifted up the coffin again, and slid it back into the bed of the truck—good as any hearse—and were off.

V

Whispering Pines Cemetery was perfectly dark. We crunched back on the labyrinth of roads and stopped at Allenade's plot. The double-wide, heart-shaped marker she'd picked out for us shining bright white in the moonlight. We climbed out of the cab shushing each other, being careful not to creak the doors. Jack took a shovel and stepped out a rectangle around the grave and then we all pitched in to carefully lift up the carpet of sod where I was supposed to lie beside my wife one day. I knew my Allenade. She'd given the coffin to me selflessly and wouldn't be at all upset if I gave it as selflessly to someone else. I knew, too, she wouldn't mind company while she waited a few more years for me to join her, and figured, with that wink she'd given me, she'd be just as happy if they laid me right down on top of her anyway.

"It's your funeral, Sam," Willie grinned.

We picked up our shovels and began to dig.

It was nearly four in the morning by the time we'd dug the hole deep enough and worked the loop of ropes to lower the casket down and piled all the dirt back on top of them and pieced the sod together again. In a day or two the grass would grow over itself, mat back together, leaving no clue. We were exhausted from saving them, but pleased with the work we'd done. Our years as widowers digging together as the Archaeological Society of Dancing Rabbit Creek had held us in good stead. The casket we'd buried held a history of love which, now that we'd discovered and buried it safely back again, could be written down to be experienced beyond the bounds of mere living. I think what we all felt for sure right then was that we hadn't come to the end of anything, but were poised to say "I do" at the threshold of our own love's journey of ten thousand years. As we gathered up our shovels and clanked like ghosts back to the truck, Willie sighed and George Chatham nodded his head. I clapped Bobby Lee on the back and Jack said, "Yep."

The Well

We keep digging. It's hot. Goddamn it's hot, and the sweat keeps getting in my eyes. But we keep digging. Me and Halsey, mindless with these shovels. I already broke one shovel. Broke it off at the handle. Johnson, he went and got it fixed, though, before I had the chance to take a smoke. I wonder about Johnson. I mean he's my boss and been my boss for the past seven years, but I still wonder.

The well we're searching for, digging up half the damn delta for, is an artesian well. That's pure drinking water that flows up of its own pressure. They say it's seventeen hundred and forty-two feet deep. Mr. Nick says that. He's retired now, but he used to work for City Water and even though this ain't City Water Mr. Nick knows what he's talking about. He says the well was first drilled back in 1904 and it's been going ever since. Now Miss Mary is getting gaps of air in the water up to the house and so we got to find the well before we call the plumbing men in to drill it back out. The well's down next to the bayou. It's on the bank of the bayou, and the mosquitoes are awful. And we're working so hard and wiping sweat we don't have time nor energy to be slapping every one of the little sonsofbitches that decides to suck out our blood. I'll tell you they're hell. God fucked up when he made mosquitoes. But the well, it's covered by a plywood kind of roof. In fact, it looks like the doors to one of them storm cellars you see out in Kansas. But this ain't Kansas and that ain't really the well. It's just the works that go to the well. Mr. Nick says the well has to be close though. And we're digging. The mosquitoes are biting like hell. Mr. Nick is standing above us on the bank with a smoke, and Johnson is squatting down looking hard at every shovelful of dirt we bring up. He's eyeing an old Coke bottle and rusted broken pipe and cinderblocks that were dumped in as filler. Saying, "Come on, boys, let's find that bitching well." And Halsey is sweating bad. I look over and the sweat is just pouring out on his black ass. He looks up and shakes his head, and drips of sweat shake off his kinky hair out from under his green cap.

"When Mr. Bob put this plumbing in," Mr. Nick says, is saying, "it was just before he died, just before the cancer took him." Mr. Nick scratches his morning beard. I see Johnson glance up at Mr. Nick. He don't like nobody talking about how Mr. Bob done things when he was alive. When Mr. Bob died, Miss Mary had hired Johnson on temporarily to oversee the farm until she could find herself a permanent manager, but then Johnson had made a good crop and she'd hired him on again. Then they'd married that second winter right after the harvest. After they'd married, we'd had to change everything so it wouldn't be like Mr. Bob had done it. He changed the time we came to work from seven o'clock to six o'clock. He changed the poison we sprayed with to Poast. He even went so far as to change the color of the shop from a rust red to an off-yellow. Johnson fired the rest of the labor that Mr. Bob had had working for him, but I was a third cousin to Miss Mary and so my job had been pretty safe. That was seven years ago. He changed everything. It wasn't that the changes were bad, just that they were changes.

"Yes, sir, some of the damndest plumbing I ever seen," Mr. Nick says and flips away his smoke. "Don't get me wrong, Bobby knew what the hell he was doing, he just had his own way of doing it." I hear Mr. Nick chuckle and then cough and spit. "That Bob was a hell of a man, a hell of a farmer." Mr. Nick goes to laughing then hacking again. "I don't guess there wasn't nothing that old boy couldn't do."

And Johnson says, "Find that bitching well, boys, come on now."

My shovel clangs metal and Halsey stops digging. I slap at the damn mosquitoes. Every time we hit metal I pray it will be the well so we can stop digging. I bend down and brush the dirt away. It's another pipe. All around us is this tangled mess of pipe, the hum of the big bullet-shaped pump set right smack in the center of them. We've already found the rust-colored overflow tank. We've already dug out from that and followed these pipes that shoot out or lead back into it. And every time we start a new direction, the first thing we've got to do is dig straight down over four feet and then widen the hole and search out from it. We've already done that, plenty.

Johnson's rooting around in the dirt at my feet. He hopped right down into the hole as soon as I struck metal. He isn't big. He's skinny and grub-white looking with thin blonde hair. He has on khakis and a short-sleeve button-down, and he never wears a cap. Mr. Bob had always worn a cap, but he was going bald from those treatments. But even before those treatments he always wore a cap. He had been a big man, heavy, and he'd get right down in the hole with you and grab up a shovel, or if we were irrigating the cotton, he'd be in the mud and the water lifting pipe and splashing right alongside us.

"It's just another goddamned pipe," Johnson says.

Mr. Nick laughs. "Yes, siree. Damndest plumbing I ever seen." He slaps his arm.

Johnson stands up and puts his hands on his hips and kind of glares at Mr. Nick. But Mr. Nick is lighting up another smoke and he don't see him. Johnson scrambles up out of the hole to squat on the edge again. He looks like a toad squatting there. "Follow that pipe," he says.

"Yes, sir," I say. I look at Halsey and Halsey looks up at me and then he shakes that sweat free again, and I wipe my face with the back of my glove, and we start digging again. My shoulders are starting to ache with the steady *thunk thunk thunk* of the shovel and then having to lift that dirt up high to dump it out on the bank. Mr. Nick comes over and looks closer into the hole. He pulls the smoke from his mouth and stares at it while he thinks. The thumb of his other hand's hooked under the strap of his overalls, his hair oiled back and these thick-rimmed black glasses with a wide strap around his head to hold them on for him.

"Boys," he says. "I do believe that's the wrong direction."

We stop digging and lean on our shovels. Halsey lights up two smokes quick and passes one to me. God it's good. I blow a cloud of smoke at the black dots hovering around me.

"I remember the day Bobby sunk the bulk of this in. I remember that like it was yesterday, but I sure as hell can't remember exactly where that well is." He slides a hand through the slick of his hair and rests his palm against the back of his neck. "But it seems to me, the well ought to follow that pipe," he says and points to one of the pipes that comes out of the overflow tank, "and go to right there." He picks up a pebble and tosses it into the hole right near the pump itself. It follows one of the pipes from the overflow tank and disappears into the dirt and part of the old cinderblock wall left surrounding the pump.

Johnson stands and stares at the place almost under the pump where the pebble landed. It made good sense to me. I look at Halsey, and he shrugs. Johnson says, "I don't believe that's it, Mr. Nick." Halsey looks at me, and I shrug.

"Well," Mr. Nick says, and drops the cigarette butt into the hole, "you can dig all day if you like, but I believe the well is there."

Johnson kind of nods. "It may be, but I got this feeling..." He don't finish it.

Mr. Nick looks at his watch. "I'm going to go get myself some lunch over to the café. These mosquitoes are like to drive me crazy. I'll stop by this afternoon some time if I get a chance." He looks at us. "See you boys later."

"I appreciate your help, Mr. Nick," Johnson says.

"Okay." Mr. Nick shakes his head as he walks over and gets in his truck. He beeps his horn and then he roars off, not even glancing sideways at us.

Johnson stares down into the hole for a long time after that, rubbing his chin. He cuts his eyes at the sun, checks it against his watch. "Let's break for lunch. Be back here at one o'clock and we'll find the bastard."

We lean our shovels against the walls of the hole and climb out. I'm covered with dirt where the sweat has made it stick.

"Mason," Johnson says to me, "take the red truck and pick up the rest of the men. Remember to be back here at one o'clock." I nod, and me and Halsey grab our coolers and carry them to the truck. Johnson still stands over the hole. It puts me in mind of a man searching down into an opened grave.

I start the truck and back it onto the road. I look beside me at Halsey. He's lighting another cigarette.

"Damn!" he says.

"I'm telling you what." I turn on the radio and drive through the green-rowed cotton fields and pick up the rest of the labor.

Johnson's already at the well when we get back at one. Maybe he didn't even go to lunch. He looks down at his watch but doesn't say anything. We climb back down into the hole. I pull on my gloves and pick up my shovel.

"There," Johnson says, "dig there." He points back toward the overflow tank to the other pipe that pokes out of it. I look at Halsey, but Halsey is looking up at Johnson. I sigh and step over the tangle of pipe and red and blue valves and stomp my shovel into the dirt. It's clay. I stomp again and pull it up. It's heavy. Halsey is working beside me as best he can. We have to start by widening the hole again. I get the pick, and that works a little better in the clay. Johnson stands on the bank and watches. I start to sweat again. We hit more broken-up cinderblock. I think how it might not have been so bad to have been fired. "Come on, Mason, dig." I look up at Johnson who's now squatting the edge and is leaning out over it to see even deeper into the hole. A cloud of mosquitoes hovers around his head, swarming him. To me, this sure as hell don't look like the pipe to the well. But I don't say word one to him.

Raking the sides with the pick, I let the dirt slide down into the hole around the pipe and Halsey shovels it out. I bite the pick in to pry off a wall, and a thick, gel-like snot shoots up into the air. I hear Johnson give a loud, "What the!" and see him stagger back from the hole. He trips on the rough clods and tumbles over backwards down the slope. The dirt he's kicked up slides down the face, leaving thirteen white snake eggs in a little hollow place tucked away in the earth. They were hiding there.

I poke one with the sharp end of the pick. It's soft and white, and they're all stuck together close as marshmallows in the heat. The one I'm poking at spurts out a greenish gob.

"What in the hell was that?" Johnson yells, stumbling back over the pile to the hole, dusting off his palms and elbows. He frowns down at his front shirt pocket which is shiny-slick where the green goop got him, and pulls a handkerchief out of his back pocket to wipe at it.

"Snake eggs," I tell him.

He stops and looks down at his handkerchief. "Are they poisonous?" He looks right at me, but I just shrug. Halsey's touching them with his shovel. He scoops them out and flips them up on the bank near Johnson's feet. Johnson leaps away.

"Watch it!"

You can't tell it by just looking, but I know Halsey got a kick out of that. Johnson peers close at the eggs, still glued together and nasty-looking. "Give me your shovel, Halsey."

Halsey hands the shovel up to him and Johnson takes it. Halsey looks at me. We both watch as Johnson presses on the eggs and rolls them about. Pokes them. He pries a couple of them apart. Bending down, he touches one with his finger. It presses in with that pressure. Soft as anything. Johnson takes a giant step back, and we watch him as he swings the shovel up high over his head. "Look out!" I yell, as he flails it down with a slap against the eggs. Snot spits everywhere from underneath the shovel blade. As I turn away I feel some of it spurt hot and wet on the back of my neck. I hear Halsey yell, "God-*damn!*" Johnson stands up over us, above us, breathing hard, the shovel all smeared with the green gunk. He peeks under it. All of the eggs are squished out. Just the skins, wrinkled flat, remain.

Johnson scrapes the shovel against the dirt, wipes it as clean as he can and hands it back to Halsey, who takes it back at arm's length. He don't say nothing; we don't say nothing neither. Halsey turns toward me, arching an eyebrow up, and then we start our digging again. We dig on that one pipe for a long time. Finally, Johnson tells us to start digging where Mr. Nick showed us.

By now it is late afternoon. The sun's long-angled through the cypress in the bayou, and the crickets are revving strong, the cicadas too. We don't talk much. I'm too damn tired to talk at all. My shirt's soaked through with old sweat and new sweat. It chills me. My whole body feels like one big itch.

Johnson stays squatted over the edge and watches. I don't believe he blinks or ever looks away. The hole is over twice the size it was when we started that morning. The dirt is piled high all around us, making the hole even deeper. Pipes lay exposed that haven't seen air for maybe eighty years, or at least since Mr. Bob fooled with them. They crisscross each other and strike out into the ground in every direction, carrying water up to Miss Mary's house and God only knows where else. The pump goes on with its even hum. Valves with blue and red and black handles poke up over the pipes they control. We keep digging.

Halsey strikes metal again. He looks at me, leaning his elbows on his knees, then up at Johnson.

"Dig it up," Johnson says.

Me and Halsey take turns at it. Both of us can't work directly on it because of the pipes that run over it and the closeness of the pump. It's a big pipe, thick. We shovel out the dirt, and then I get down on my hands and knees so I can brush and scoop out the dirt around the turn in the neck of the pipe with my hands. I see the "W" on the big bolt in the valve where it turns straight down.

I look back at Johnson. He's squatted there. It seems he's hovering over the hole. His eyes stare at my hands on the well. They're wide open and unblinking. He sways with his intensity. I nod, "It's the well, Mr. Johnson." He still stares, staring, and then he lets out this big breath. He breaks his eyes from the well and blinks out over our heads. Then he looks off toward the house.

"Right," he says. "All right. That's a day. Go on and pick up the rest of the men. I'll call the plumbers tonight and tomorrow, first thing, we'll rip this entire mess out and do it right."

Me and Halsey collect the shovels and the pick and climb up out of the hole. We lug all of the tools to the truck and dump them in the bed. I watch Johnson still squatting over the hole. I start the truck and throw my arm over the seat to back out onto the road, turn and face forward again in time to see Johnson jump down into the hole and disappear. I glance over at Halsey, watching too. He leans back and blows smoke. "Um," he says, and flicks his ash out the window. I drive out slow till I hit the corner, and then I put the pedal to the floor.

McCommas

Randolph

I'm standing by the bar in the Lighthouse, and Georgia's sitting back there on her red stool sipping her mix of Jack and Falls City from a tea cup, and there's some Hank going— yodelling out the blues like—when in strolls Big Ephraim Pelfrey. My arms go immediately tight, and I'm wondering right away what's the fucking deal and cut my eyes to my brothers, Daniel and Andrew, and our cousin Evil Vance is with us and he's a big man—only McCommas near big as Big Eph Pelfrey—and he's all a-frown. You can tell right away that Big Eph is thinking he like to made a mistake, and big as he is, huge, I see the slow step he takes into the bar, not at all sure he wants to do what he's doing but doing it anyway, his hand still kind of holding the doorknob ready to beat hell out of there and his little Pelfrey pig eyes blinking little stupid pig blinks against the smoke and darker black of the bar air and the music going. And me thinking, *What in the hell?* Because he knows we are going to be here because we are always here if we're not home or fishing or hunting or out on the tug. *What in the hell?* because I sure as hell wouldn't go into town and set a foot in Maxine's Lounge with all the Pelfreys living there, not for love nor money, but here is Big Eph and he is standing in our place.

The pool balls are quiet against the felt, and when Hank quits singing you can hear the arm of the player lift, and the next record slip and drop and spin, and the crackling, and then *A Country Boy Can Survive*. Ephraim's eyes are darting all over the place, and I can see them going like quick minnows in a pool, and so I stand up from my stool and call to him real loud and clear.

"Ephraim," I say and hold up my beer.

His eyes stop on mine, and I can see him thinking that if he was smart he'd get the hell out of here, but he ain't smart, and he lets go of the doorknob and takes a giant step in. He skirts my brothers at the pool table, and Evil Vance gives him a stare, but Big Eph don't take it up in here like I know he would if were were at any other spot in this entire county. Ephraim's eyes are still going, and it's then I see he's looking for someone. He must want them bad too, more than his goddamn life to be in here. And of a sudden I'm thinking, *Goddamn, who?* and wondering. He steps up to the bar.

"Randolph."

I nod for Georgia to draw us both a beer. She squints up her gash of a face like there's some by-Jesus God-awful stank in the room, so I have to take my eyes off Eph, which I do not want to do even for this second, and stab her with a look which says, *Just do like I tell you, old woman, goddamnit.* She bangs our mugs down like a kid for having to. Eph picks up the beer, and I can see this smile just break his bottom lip as he nods thanks, and for a second I can almost smile with him and like him a bit, like him like I maybe would if he was any man but a Pelfrey and we were sitting here just drinking. Then I remember again about what his grandaddy did to my grandaddy's sister and what my grandaddy had to do to him, and my daddy dead from it all, too, eventually, and what my uncles had to do then to Ephraim's daddy, raking the hot coals hotter. And I think how me and Ephraim are both the oldest and how we have grown up with it together now for over thirty years, fifteen without dropping it. I think of his brother, Emanuel, and some of my cousins, and all the other fights at dances and knives pulled at the election polls and other shit too, going long back, the way it has always been and will always be between the McCommases and the Pelfreys in these hills, and I can hate him again then, easy. I don't even have to try. He kills the draft, smears the back of his hand across his beard, and sets the mug down. I nod for Georgia to hit him again.

"'Preciate it."

We're both watching Georgia's small hands on the black-and-gold tap of Black Label. She has a ring of some sort on every finger and three or even four jangle her ring finger, which we always say are for all her boyfriends and husbands, McCommases somehow, though the way she used to get around I wouldn't doubt a Pelfrey or two in the woodpile somewheres. There's a picture of two pigs screwing on the wall, and under it, it says, "MAKING BACON!" An orange Strohs light glows neon, and in the old dresser mirror propped on the counter I can keep the edge of my eye on me and Big Eph sitting side by side.

Eph turns to me and draws one finger slow across his lip. Practically all you can see of his face is this wild tangle of beard and in it this one raw strip of lip and, if he talks, which he don't much, the black rot of his teeth. He rests his big elbows on the bar, and his stomach strains his Harley buckle to popping. His arms are the size of stolen ham hocks hidden in the sleeves of his jean jacket. I ain't scared of him, though, and never have been, 'cause I am good and fast with a blade and even sharper with a rifle, and Eph knows it too.

"Cold as hell out there."

I nod to that. "Ice's this thick out on the Guyandotte," I say and hold my hands about two feet apart.

Eph shakes his head. "Goddamn. Probably snow again tonight too."

"I imagine. Warning for a storm."

We're kind of half-sitting, half-standing, leaning against the bar, and the pool game is clacking on, but I can tell neither Daniel nor Andrew nor Vance got their minds on their cutthroat, just waiting to back me up. One sign, for Budweiser, cocked in the window, is red flashing on and off like a hanging stop or a caution.

"Mary been in tonight?"

My beer stalls on my lips. Then I make myself swallow and then I make myself set the mug down. In the mirror Big Eph ain't looking at me. He's looking at his hands, turning my eyes there—creviced with the coal dust which I can imagine too making black sandbags of his lungs. It's true there was a time when our families ran together and even intermarried through these hills, but nobody alive except my Great Mamaw Elizabeth is able to remember that, and her just a kid then, and now she's so old that she's dead really except for bumping into things and sogging her gums together and this flashlight which winks on and off about a hundred times in the middle of the night. True, too, we even had some McCommases down in the mines for a time, and in the UMW, but now the Pelfrey's got the mines and the town—and can have them both—and we own the rivers, which go all the way out to the living Ohio. I think what kind of people they are that can live like moles without the wind and spray and light of the sun, and I am glad I am not one of them.

I take it all this slow, scratch around inside my ear, inspect the wax under my nail. "Mary who?" I say.

"Mary McCommas," he says, and meets me in the mirror.

"That's right, Ephraim," I say, holding his eyes. "You got that right. *McCommas.*"

There don't seem like nothing else for us to say, and we are sitting there like that, and then he goes for his pocket and the whole place fucking explodes—Vance pinning him from behind and Daniel coming in two-fisted with the butt of his pool cue, the slit of Andrew's Buck knife. Eph don't fight it or nothing, his hand caught there in the air where it didn't quite make it to his pocket. His pig eyes don't tell me a damn thing, but I nod to Vance anyway, who shrugs him loose. Big Eph's hand continues down, and I'm watching it and not watching too, my eyes never leaving his eyes and his eyes never leaving mine, and he picks out his wallet, which is chained to his belt loops, and takes out two one-dollar bills and spreads them flat on the counter.

"Keep the change," he says, and winks at Georgia, and then he swivels on his stool, nods to me, and stands up. I see now he is even bigger than Evil Vance, because he gives him a good stare down, and Vance says, "Why you mother-fucker," and tries to rush him backwards, but I stop him with my voice and by how sharp and cold I say it so he knows I'm not fucking around, and he lets Ephraim walk out. The wind bites in, and then the door booms shut, and we all watch Big Eph stride by the flashing Budweiser, flipping up the sheepskin collar on his coat. Waylon winds it down, and I turn back to my beer. I grab a quarter and step toward the jukebox, roll my twenty-five cents in, and punch J6 for *Rocky Top*. The banjo races in, and I call Georgia for a round of beers. Then Daniel slaps Vance on the back and says, "I thought you was going to whup his ass, son." And Andrew laughs shrill, like he does, and Vance gives a whoop. "God*damn!*"

I walk over and sit back down on my stool.

Georgia shakes her head and wipes across the counter. "That Pelfrey boy's got balls though." She smiles. "You got to admit that."

"Yep," I say, and I mean it. He does, and I respect that. But while Georgia foams my beer, I am thinking how much trouble there is going to be, fully considering the size of Ephraim Pelfrey's balls and what it took for him to drag them in here, into the Lighthouse, and ask for my sister. I look up and see that it has already started to snow outside. I think how I'll need something stronger than beer to get me through this night. I ask Georgia for the phone, thinking how I should first call Mary.

MARY

"Nope," I say. Shake my head. "Ain't no way." Shriver's sending up this panic at the phone's jangling, but I leave it ring, cannot possibly imagine anyone I want to talk to about anything tonight. I try to toss it off, to be as bullish as I pretend to myself I've always been about men, saying, *Them that live by the sword die by it*. This'd usually strike me as pretty funny, but tonight it runs me straight through the heart home, sobers me to thinking how my mind was made up for me a long time ago, before I had a chance or a choice or was goddamn born even.

I trace my fingernail around the lip of my glass, look up as if I'd just sat down, wondering how in the hell I got out here on this porch in the first place anyhow, brooding down on the wreck of home lights which're the town of Guyandotte and the spark-red warnings of the tugs out to the Ohio too: my life. Snowing like mad out. I recognize how I'm getting a little drunk perhaps and how I'm pretty glad I'm finally getting drunk enough to do what has to be done and I let that phone go on and on just a ringing like that, wishing myself to consider about anything else for a time.

My brothers built this porch for me—this perch high up on this hawk's nest ridge—though I never asked them to build it for me nor paid one penny for it and'd pay to have it tore down in a half-second if I thought it meant I owed them anything. They just showed up one October Saturday morning with their hammers and electric saws and a truckload of lumber from Lowes. I woke with He Man rolling on the tube and my mouth dead-dry and the Cuervos and too many cigarettes from the night before stuck stinking on the back of my tongue, Randolph's face pressed up against the screen like some stockinged robber's, sandy hair curling out from under his cap worn bill backwards.

"Rough night, huh, Sis," he said, laughing, and I rolled up off the couch and bundled the sleeping bag close against my nakedness and almost fell down. I unlatched the screen and Randolph barged in and pecked me on the cheek. Andrew and Daniel and Vance were with him too, outside squatting around the truck like he'd probably ordered them, and before I could ask, Randolph smiled and said, "Going to build that porch for you." Then the saws were humming and whir-buzzing and planks dropping, lopped off. I fixed coffee and bacon and sausage and eggs and muffins and took it out to them, and they ate quick and hunched over and without talking, serious like they always ate summers I'd worked cooking for them out to the tug, serious and hunched over

and busy with it, like eating was a kind of job too, and then
went straight back to work again.

I needed four black cups myself just to face a shower, letting the water run down over me and scrubbing good,
holding my mouth open to the spray, slushing and spitting
it out. Back in the bedroom, I touched the flat of my stomach in the mirror, ran the flat of my palms down over my
good hips, but my mind so swole up already big with it that
I dressed in my fattest pair of Lees and taller-heeled boots
and one of Randolph's old baggy flannel shirts before I
risked going back out there to watch them again. At noon
I fixed twelve roast beef sandwiches and swirled up three
pitchers of Lipton's. By evening the porch was finished, railing and all, except for the painting, which I haven't done
and know I'll never do for myself now, and we sat on the
bare planks and drank Millers. And sitting there, sipping
the good beers, humming along with Andrew playing his
guitar and singing quietly in his good gentle voice,

I can feel the sweet winds blowing
through the valleys and the hills—
I can feel the sweet winds blowing
as I go, as I go.

I almost felt like their sister again. Almost—though I
knew the whole thing must've been Randolph's idea. The
rest of them had had it up to here with me, and fine with
me, too, just how I'd planned my life and how I'd always
wanted to live it, separate from being a McCommas. Why I'd
moved away from the rivers and up to this trailer on this
ridge in the first place. I'd done exactly what I knew I had
to do to divorce myself from them, thinking of the fights I'd
heard they were getting into over me, how I said, *Fuck
that*—their problem, not mine. I felt Randolph watching me

then, and I tugged my shirttails baggy down around myself and got up to get another round of beers. I slapped back of the screen, Andrew picking his way straight into "Mountain Stream."

You'd better listen to the voices from the mountains—
trying to tell you what you just might need to know.

And knowing, listening. Looking in turn at each of my brothers—Randolph, Daniel, Andrew, and my cousin Vance—the fuckers.

The phone stops. Takes a long breath. Then starts in to ringing again.

"Just leave me alone, you goddamn sons of a bitches!" I scream, stumbling up to fire my glass at the box wall of snow, but it don't shatter nor even break nor anything at all, making me feel weak and helpless and out of control, which I can't never stand. I don't even hear it land—smothered under the sky avalanche-weight of snow—just Shriver crying and digging crazy at the back door.

I lurch over and yank open the screen. Shriver worms out and shoves his nose straight into my crotch. "Not you too," I say and knee past him and on into the kitchen, brushing snow out of my long hair, soaking, off my shoulders. I blink the wet from my eyelashes, reach up and take down another tumbler, and pour out a stiff one. Then I follow Shriver's wagging balls down the hall and into the bedroom. The phone stops ringing, sharper than it began, this sudden quick quiet. I pick up the receiver and listen to the dead buzzing. I hang it up, set the Jack down on the bedside table, and go straight to the closet. I slide open the door and kneel down, rummage under my dirty-clothes basket. Rise up with the Remington 1100.

The goddamn truth—as I sink the rubber butt of the

shotgun down on the waterbed and tilt open the green-and-yellow box of double-X buckshot shells on the dresser—the goddamn truth and realization of it all I know now's that all I've really managed to do's go and royally screw myself. Thinking how the only thing I despise more than all these men's myself and the web trap of this McCommas life I was born to die in.

I peel five shells off the top row and slide them one by one into the chamber. The plug's out and it takes all five. I *shlang* the metal back. It won't take me that long, I don't guess, and I leave the bedroom light on and tuck the shotgun under my arm. Shriver comes up sniffing again and I crack him a good one across the skull with the barrel which sends him a yelping. I shove out of the trailer. Turn and throw the bolt behind me.

EPHRAIM

I hike my way on out the hideaway cut. On and up the white road to where her bright trailer sets parked. I step straight on up to the door and pull open the screen. I try the knob, but it is locked. I knock, and that dog goes off, barking, but Mary don't come to the door. "Honey," I says, and then I says it louder but still softly, so that she will know it is me, *"Darling?"* I let the screen slap back and step over the hedge to take a peek in her bedroom—where I have loved being, though now I am turned out. That black dog looks back at me from in there, and then it yips and grins at me with its teeth, gums quivering back. She has been here, though, since I drove by last not two hours ago. The light is on and a bra and red panties lay pooled up on the floor where they slid off her, her stockings hung over the door. I feel that sure and I miss her even more now, if that is possible. My face is so close that I believe I can smell her sweet perfume and the smothered stale of her Vantage cigarettes. But it must be the strength of my strong wishing, 'cause they is only that empty crystal cold of the wet and snow.

I leave the window. Then I suddenly see how stupid I have been—her lights're on but her Monte Carlo's gone. The tire tracks of her leaving is dulled with snow, but still holding sharp at the pressed edges, and so I know I have just missed her. Looking now, I can see she drove down off the backside of the mountain. Maybe she is out hunting for *me*, I think, and we is just going shy of each other every-wheres we go. I think to check the back door—like I have walked in some nights when she has called me and wanted me and has been waiting on top of the covers. Then I see headlights winding up toward the trailer, slow because of the slick. My heart gives a rise, but then I think, *What if it ain't Mary at all, but Randolph or one of them old boys?* And I think how they have seen more than enough of Ephraim Pelfrey for one night.

I pull away from the window and slide on down behind the side of the trailer where I can see peeking out but can't be seen. The car is a truck and it's got chains on against the ice, ching-changing and fishtailing the last turn as it comes up. *Randolph.* He pulls into the drive and throws it into park. He leaves the engine running and the lights on too and hops out. He jumps up the front steps and bangs the door, which sets that dog off again. I hear him rattle the knob. Then he leaves it and hurries on around back, and I slide down the hill on the opposite side. Get to the corner in time to see him step onto the porch and try that door—that dog howling like all hell's been busted into—and it is open. He don't bother to stamp off his boots. Goes right in without bothering to catch the door.

I scramble on back up the hill, fall, slick as anything, and get up brushing snow. Make it to the bedroom window in time to see him come straight into the lamplight. I am watching between the crack of shade and windowsill, but my breath is fogging even that up for me, so that I have go to circle it away with the tips of my blue-feeling fingers, careful not to squeak it. Randolph picks a glass up off the bedside table and smells it—half amber-clear like whiskey— then he kicks the drink back.

He stands there like that with the empty glass in his hand and then he sees her panties. He bends down and picks them up, holds them in front of him in the air and then lays them gently on the foot of her waterbed. I watch him as his eyes click around for more clues and catch on a box of double-X Winchester shotgun shells on the edge of the dresser, the orange $8.99 Kmart price tag still stuck on them. He picks them up—ain't a foot away from me now at the dresser—and they is something on his face as he sets them down again, sets the glass down that quick too, and then he goes straight for the closet. It is open and he kneels there under her dresses and she has got about a million pair of shoes stacked up there above. Just seeing the things that get to touch her about kills me. This aching. He comes up from kneeling empty-handed. Then he is out of the room— that quick—and I hear him shaking through the house, the back door slamming before I have a chance to slide back down there and check. And then he is trotting out to his truck and hops in and shoves it into reverse, this one wind-shield wiper fending off all the snow as he whirs it back and then stops, fishtails forward and is gone, taillights winking red as he taps the brakes going down, the engine whining as he slows the slide into first.

I head straight for the porch. Randolph's left his foot-prints in the snow, but I can see where someone else has been sitting out here tonight, less than an inch of fresh snow on the lawn chair. Six, seven inches total piled on the rail. I grab the knob, hoping, but it is locked. He didn't even bother to shut the door going in, but he has locked it going out behind him again. I stand up into the snow snowing down, just breathing deep to myself—shut out again this far away, out in the cold and separate from her, like it seems I always am. If I think of her too much like this when she ain't around, I am lost and go crazy. I think how I am crazy without her.

I glance at my watch, already past one o'clock. I think how she could have got called into work. But then I remember her stockings and her two miniskirt uniforms hung up with the rest of her dresses in the closet where I looked over them. Then it strikes me again that maybe Mary is circling all around hunting for me like I am a hunting for her, and we is just missing each other everywhere we go, like in a movie. I think how she knows I am down to Maxine's or at the bowling alley parking lot, same as I always am with my brothers of an evening, how what I should really do instead of hounding her all around like this is just go there and just sit and wait for her to find me now. Then maybe we can come back up here together and I will pop the question like I have been chasing around and around in a sweat to ask her. I reach in my pocket and finger the ring. In my mind, hoping this will prove to her how serious I am this time, thinking like I have rehearsed it again and again, *Will you please marry me?* Then I remember how it is my brothers will sure be looking for me too. It is late and they might be stuck outdoors with nowheres else to go. And I hope she will look to find me now, because I have done all I can do.

My brothers ain't at Maxine's. I cruise by and find them bundled up in the back parking lot of the Colonial Lanes. I park and throw the doors open wide to them. Smile.

"Evening, gentlemen."

"Evening, Eph," Elijah nods, stomping the cold off before he climbs in.

My cousin, Elias, shakes his head. "Thought you'd never get here, son. 'Bout froze to death waiting."

And Ezra says, "Missed you to Maxine's."

"Had some things I had to take care of," I tell them. "Got here soon's I could."

Elijah whistles as he settles in, hugging himself. "Only a madman'd be out driving around in this stuff."

"Hey," I says, and open up my palms, which gets a pretty good laugh from them.

I reach out and pull the doors closed, lock down the latches—already warmer—feeling good to be this close and piled in and all together again and how it always is with me and my brothers.

Five minutes ain't passed before I catch the first stuttered purr of Ezra's snoring. This gurgled chorus as Elijah and my Cousin Elias join him. I grin thinking how I will ride hell out of them for it as we rumble the mantrip deep into 2B tomorrow morning. Then I hear the snow-muffled engine. Cut my eyes at my watch. It is a quarter to two o'clock and there is a car out idling in our parking lot.

I touch the ring—a last hope. Then I pat over the carpet and grab up a monkey wrench. Can't never be too sure, and especially not tonight, with Randolph McCommas buzzing around after I shook up that hornet's-nest Lighthouse. I cock the wrench at the scrunching of footsteps. But then I hear the quiet knock—three times halt and then one, like only she knows is our Pelfrey code. And then her soft-voiced whisper, calling me to her, *"Ephraim."*

"Honey?" I says quiet, checking my brothers' steady snoring. "Is that you, Darling?" I whisper and lay my weapon back down on the carpet. I kneel carefully forward

and unlatch the back doors for her. Throw them open wide to welcome my bride-to-be in out of the storm.

Georgia

I wake to the goddamndest pounding on the downstairs door, and I get up and creep to the window and slit the curtains to look out to see who the crazy person is standing there banging it. "Well, my Lord," I say. See it is Mary McCommas, without a hat on or even a coat, standing out there in that snow, and so I wrap on my pink silk kimono and tread downstairs. I peek open the door, and she pushes right in.

"I need your help," she says.

"Randolph's been trying to call you all—"

And she says, "I've been out."

I just look at her then and at first I don't get it at all, and she just keeps staring, her face so white and expectant-looking, and then I say, "My God, you mean you're—"

"Yeah," she says and runs her fingers back through her wet hair.

"You're soaking wet. Let me—"

"Are you going to help me or not?" The way she says it and the way she looks, all scary wide-eyed like a horse in a barn fire, I am afraid she is going to run back out into the snow.

"Sure, honey. I mean if you're sure and all. I mean if you're sure about the father and—"

"Fuck the father." And then she laughs too short and hard, and I take another real good look at her, because it is a laugh I myself have had and I know a lot of girls who have it or have gotten it, and though she is a wild bucking one, I did not think she would ever be one of us. Then she stops laughing and says real calm, "I'm sure about the father. I made sure about the father."

I nod. Lots of girls come to me late in the night. That's when I do my best business and it does not surprise me to have someone banging on my door past two A.M. What does surprise me is that Randolph and Ephraim Pelfrey are both out there looking for Mary, and that she is right here talking to me on my doorstep, and that she is pregnant. Her face is hard and white, her cheeks pinched sharp by the wind, and I am beginning to puzzle this story together for myself.

"Sure," I say. "If you're sure, honey, I am." I wave her into the back room behind the bar where I store the boxes of liquor and where I do a fairly good tattoo business in the afternoons. There is an old kitchen table and one chair. "You'll want to take your clothes off. Here's a towel to wrap yourself in."

I turn my back on her while she strips, and start to remove each of my rings. I drop them one by one into a styrofoam cup, and as I take them off I like to remember where I got each one, each of these men. Then I soap my hands and wash them off—a kind of virgin again. I turn back to her and she is sitting naked on the table. She is shivering and her nipples are up, swollen to a deep purple.

"Those are some nice boobs you got," I say and I smile to take the edge off things. "I used to have a pair of them myself that got me into some trouble once or twice." She doesn't smile at that, and I take a bottle out of one of the boxes and twist the label and hand it to her, thinking to loosen her up and also of what is to come. "You might want a sip of this."

"No," she says.

I shrug to that and pour a dollop in my teacup. "Suits me." Mary is laying there naked with her legs spread and her nipples bruised up, and I think how maybe I ought to call Randolph before I do anything too permanent. "You want I should call Randolph or Daniel or Andrew or Vance, maybe, or somebody?" By *somebody,* meaning Ephraim Pelfrey, of course. Her head is turned away, and she is staring at the opposite wall. "Mary?" I say.

She shakes her head. "Call Randolph," she says. "After."

I nod. It is really none of my business, and if she wants it done, that is good enough for me. No man's keeper. "Okay. I'll call Randolph after."

I turn back to the sink and snap on a pair of latex gloves, humming.

> *Don't you want to go to that land?*
> *I'm a-going to go to that land.*
> *Don't you want to go to that land where I go?*

All the while thinking about the evening at the Lighthouse—about Big Ephraim Pelfrey strolling in. I kind of smile remembering the wink he gave me. Them Pelfrey boys have got balls. I'll give them that. Though these McCommases ain't soft, and Mary is lying here to prove it. I reach down and touch the white insides of her thighs, feel her shudder like horseflesh under my fingertips.

"Don't worry now, Honey," I tell her. "You won't hardly feel this a bit."

Crow Man

And Rarden then whining down over the border oaks, swooping down that stick, flapping rudders, to hop, skip, jump down over those trees and trailing poison out of his wings, six long thin streams over twelve rows of cotton, and him so low his wheels go to brushing the bolls, a *thup-thup-thup* sound like the queen of hearts stuck in the spoke of my now grandson's bike, and his great double-winged eagle shadow bunched down so small underneath or to either side depending on the time of the summer sun. Straight up and down noon when he would spray out the last of his load, shoot his wad, as he used to say, and buzz back to Legion Field and land and then throw me his goggles and leather helmet, which he wore but of course didn't have to, and jump in his truck and head for Nadine's.

Nadine's where Naomi was, who he called Felicity Jane, and him being from the North and her some breed of Chickasaw, Choctaw, probably Negro, mixed-up kind of blood, cheekbones high and silent, but a strong and questionable nose, and wider lips than maybe she had a right to as just an Indian, and a kink to her hair which was unexplainable any other way.

The truth of the whole thing being he, Rarden, scared the shit out of people whether he was looping and swoop-diving almost crash in that plane, an old barnstorming Jenny, or at Nadine's, drinking Dixie beer or any whiskey they had, and just after twelve noon, too, or before even, it didn't matter to him. There to see Naomi, saying *Good afternoon, Miss Felicity Jane,* like he was a cowboy or something and this in Mississippi, and, of course, her never saying nothing, and not even hardly raising her eyes.

But it was her that shot him. Nobody else had to do it. Killed him, I believe, like you would stomp the head off a wing-crippled mockingbird. And everybody always used to say there wasn't no need to shoot him even if there was a need to, because the way he piloted that plane, he was quick on his way to hell anyway. If you ever heard a boom of lightning-flash thunder, first you thought it was old Rarden done bought his ticket, done gone home, but then it never was, and he became a kind of legend like some nine-foot Jesus, gained a reputation, see, for being crazy, and so for the most part people left him alone, just shook their heads and waited for him to die, which of course, he did, just not like they expected.

The water tower stood up like a silver head, winking in the sunlight, and as I yanked back the stick and bellied by it, the ground dropped and became blue way-up sky and away and then spinning under and back, rotating blue, green, brown where it should be, and I could read where he'd painted her name, red, candy-apple red, FELICITY JANE, over

the kid signs OLD MISS REBELS, CLASS OF '25, JOEY C. LOVES
S.M., and older rain-streaked and year-faded loves and
cheers. There for anybody who wanted to see. FELICITY JANE.
Rolling that old Jenny over and spraying back through Mr.
Sutton's fields close by my last tissue marker, and then
empty-light and streaking straight back to Legion Field,
where Rarden would be looped and feeling high, ready to fly,
to be up, after his whiskey lunch and beer and seeing Naomi.
He'd tell me how fine she was. *Something.* And already wearing his leather helmet and goggles, and the quick choke
snort as the prop died, and dust by our shack at the airfield
rose and fell in the different same place, not mattering, and
him, Rarden, strolling out with that big smile on his face.
And Jasper, he'd say to me, *she is so fine. I never met a woman
like that before.* Me thinking that he probably had, but that
because I was thinking of what kind of Mary Magdalene
woman I thought she was and not what he thought she was.
Fueling, and him up again, in love and flying, which is what
he did, like some men walk or run, or go into business. He
fell in love and flew. He just drank on the side.

It was Rarden taught me to fly. Nobody else could see a nigger in the air. But me. I could see it and wanted it so bad, I
could chew it like gristle, and toted gas and loaded chemi-
cals for it, and don't think nobody would never have let me
up but crazy Rarden. *Hey, Jasper,* those low-ground niggers
at the café say, *Hey Crow man. Crow. You want to fly?* he
said, grinning ear to ear, those goggles on and dusted so he
had to clear them with his finger. *Sho',* I said. And him
being from the North, Ohio or some such place, laughed,
and then was a cowboy again from someplace else again,
misplaced again, like he always was, a square peg in a round
hole, laughing, and talking like me, saying *sho' nuf?* Put me
in the cockpit and took me up. *Born with wings,* he yelled

over the hum-rush-buzz of air, me already with the stick. And it was true. After leaving that old ground, there wasn't nothing else I ever wanted to do. Like an angel. Couldn't go back to just being some no-count field nigger no more. 'Cause I been to heaven. I seen that light. A *goddamned natural,* he said, and made me his partner right on the spot, even though I told him I didn't have no money and couldn't afford to buy no stock, and he just looked at me. It was true he didn't have no idea what I was talking about and didn't want a dime.

Of course, De La Palma owned her, and there never was a chance for them. Owned her not like a slave and like a slave, like a rich man owns a Choctaw Chickasaw probably nigger that nobody else does and maybe can't get a job but that she's good-looking and quiet and was willing or didn't think enough of it not to go down on her back. But you couldn't tell that to Rarden. He'd just snort and take a drink and offer me the bottle, and I'd take a swig and pass it back, and him not bothering to even swipe the lip with his sleeve. That was the kind of man he was. This after work, fourteen hours of spraying, flying, and flying the thing between us, air, sky, blue, and we both could have used more, and us both sitting in our shack, with our partner name, R & J, for Rarden and Jasper, fresh-painted on the door. Crop dusters just plain too long and so we left it off.

Fine, he'd say about her, *fine.* Dreamy-like.

And me thinking there wasn't no chance in hell and saying that she was Mr. De La Palma's girl like everybody knew and nobody said or wanted to know just how, like the devil owns souls. He even owned Nadine's, though everybody said it was Nadine's. But it was his jack that kept the place going. But saying to Rarden, *She's just a plain girl. Just a girl. Ain't got no people, ain't go no home.*

Felicity Jane? You talking about Felicity Jane. And this frowning, whiskey-thinking look at me. This kinda crazy look. He was crazy. And he was sane too.

And I'd say, *Well*. And leave it at that.

Now she lives down over the Hushpuckashaw River, in a little cabin there, the trestle bridge rising over and above her, still on De La Palma's land, though De La Palma dead and been dead twenty years and never touched her after she turned thirty no ways. I see her sometimes snapping beans into a bright Indian-looking apron. Her gray hair long down her back, like a cape down her back, earned these fifty years since. But we don't talk about him. Though maybe we should, both of us being so old now, over for us, and Rarden being the best and worst thing that ever happened to either one of us. The only real free man, white or black or Indian, crazy or sane, that I ever seen. And for her too. I'm sure of that. Not De La Palma.

It was both of them that climbed the water tower. Together. Arm over arm, hand over hand, up that Jacob's ladder. To the top. And him toting that candy-apple-red red paint and a brush. It was the same brush he used to paint our partner name, R & J. Up and up. Until they were up there standing and laughing and no doubt drinking, because there was that between them too, or not between but *with* them—and still all that way to go back down—but Rarden I know didn't care because he, like any bird, was totally disregardless of heights, and she too, like me, was more natural and alive in the air, and so had no fear of dying that way. Wings. Angels. Crows. Eagles. And I wonder how he saw that in us? What he saw in us? A nigger and a Chickasaw Choctow half-breed nigger too? What was it about us that he picked out? And how did we fall back to this man and woman's ground again? 'Cept that we were out of place as him. And him from a kind of place like Ohio? But he did pick us. But maybe, too, it was us picked him. And he took that brush out, and I can see them now, up there, kissing, her breasts filling up that beaded shirt, and her long lightish colt legs under her one skirt, and swiping that brush across that tower in huge arm-sweeping candy-apple-red letters, big, FELICITY JANE. The town unable to escape it, obvious now, even to De La Palma.

De La Palma was not one of these Southern sheriffs you see on TV, and Rarden didn't hate him, not really, and he, De La Palma, got us more business, more fields—maybe just to increase the odds, more air time, more time for crashing. Give him time. Let God take care of it. He will, you know. But he got the fields for us, and we were thankful. Us flying from dusk 'til dawn to dusk again. Until it was even too much for us, much as I liked to take my turns. So Naomi quit Nadine's, and her too now, up. Rotating in and out. That old Jenny whining, humming, thrumming up and up, swooping down, raining pellets to fight that old red vine, that nasty bo' weevil, all them things which creep up on man's cotton. And she was good. More than I. Both of us flying. All three of us flying high. Money. We had more money than what we knew to do with, 'cause Rarden didn't want it, see. He just didn't want it. Or if he took some and used it, it wasn't like he cared about it or was hoarding it. And that was the pure thing or what made it the purest thing, flying. And at night, one oil lantern, and the shadows playing happy with his face, and he was good and the best doing what it was he did, and maybe touching Naomi's leg, playing with the fringe of her Indian kind of jacket, beads, and laughing. Drinking. And going up tomorrow. Seven days a week. Asking, *Why should you rest when you're doing what you*

want to do? Why should anything keep you out of the air?
Nothing, man, I'd say, I'm saying. *Nothing.*

From there, the water tower, God's perch, the whole town
laid out like something you could read, like something you
could understand, like a map maybe: FELICITY JANE and the
silver rail tracks, north-pulsing glints of sunshine, and the
little block town, and the then two-lane 46 highway, and
quilt fields like red, brown, green, greener, greenest
swatches of cloth and pieced together with the stitching
boarder of trees. And the trestle bridge, which was an old
one, in fact used to swivel to let steamboats through, but not
any more, crossing the Hushpuckashaw River and just high
enough. Just. Barely just. And like a final test of knowing
your craft, coming down up humping the reaching oaks,
and then slick slide like a fair ride, and scooting down close
to the water, taking the slow curve bend, and then there,
suddenly, the bridge, and just enough to clear the wheels,
sppppiiiittttttzzzzz, dragging the current, the sound of zip-
ping fishing line trawled by a fast boat, and the wings on
either side inches from the bricks, and your legs warm,
weak, and weary, wonderful like after loving, and hand
gentle fine, and squeaking out, and another curve, and a
kind of hop back on the stick, ballsy barnstorming, and up
over, leaning back, and the fingers of that gravity tickling
you out, upside down, rolling all the way over and loop
once, sliding long back over the field and out, safe, and
screaming the best thing you ever done. I seen him do it a
hundred times. I done it three. Naomi done it every time she
got the chance. And him in the back sometimes too, just riding, drinking, both hands in the air, trusting her.

Free. That's all any of us can hope for. And Rarden was. No
strings. Flying. Making love. Drinking. Up and up. The only

free man, white or black or anything, that I ever made the acquaintance of. Knew the real value of time and money—which is nothing unless it's to buy and have the afternoon and evening to drink whiskey—and was willing to pass on the gift of flight, or let you know if you had it, to touch you with the chance, which was enough and all anybody can ask for, didn't want to hang on to it for himself. Because Rarden was what he was. No explanations for that. And I can't explain why, because that would be like saying why something fly and something else don't. When it flies it's good enough. Fly it.

But Naomi. FELICITY JANE. Choctaw. Chickasaw. Nigger. Probably white. But she grew up black, or as good or bad as black. Outside of town. On De La Palma's place, and that's where De La Palma found her. Raised her, really, when, I'm sure, he saw her potential for beauty. And she was beautiful in that way of mixing which had come out somehow right, and the good strong features of four separate peoples giving her something nobody else—something nobody else woulda even chosen, given the choice—but she had it. Silent as an Indian and as thoughtful. She would laugh, those nights spent in our shack drinking and talking flying, which was the only thing to talk, R & J & FJ now on the door—he couldn't call her just Felicity or just Jane and never Naomi, and she didn't even seem to mind or even care what he called her, not in a bad way, but like an Indian, as if she was who she was and a name didn't catch her no ways, like naming the "wind"—but her laugh was just a smile, thin-lipped, real, but reserved, and it was only when flying that I saw her really break it out, sparkling, beautiful.

But I'm thinking something about the end, why she killed him. Because De La Palma owned her? Owned her as much as the land, the soil and earth what made her and so could never be free from that? Or that she was free enough for a moment to free him, the best and kindest way, and a hell of a thing too? And so I am thinking about being free. What is it about being set free? What is it about setting someone free? Making me think, again, now and all these past fifty years, *And what does free mean?*

She was up, her turn, out spraying, and we were sitting in our partner shack, the smell of gasoline, and Poast 316, and lime too, and the radio going on K96, playing, feet up, whiskey between us, the hot taste of fertilizer and dust still in my mouth from my own flight, almost lunchtime. When then a choke and gurgle spit sputter and out the door us already scanning the sky for the Jenny and then saw her worbling in too low to clear the power and telephone wires, and then *No!* and the wheels snagged, caught, growl and snatched out of the air like swiping a fly, yanked out of the air, swung down around it, wrapped in the wire, buzzing, crackle, *BANG!* of the transformer and sizzling electricity, popping, and us both running, the plane hung from the wires by its tail like a condemned man from the rope, like a giant trophy fish, engine dead, and Naomi there slung down, arms out, and Rarden saved her, chinned up onto the propellor, shimmied up to the cockpit and pulled her out, unconscious, and lowered her down, and no sooner all of us on the ground when the wires snapped and the Jenny crumpled, nose first, into the ground.

That was the end of R & J & FJ. We had money but not enough for another plane. Rarden even went to De La Palma. De La Palma said he wished he could help us. He *wished* he could.

An angel on the ground, though maybe still an angel, is lacking. She no longer has that something which makes her special. An eagle on the ground ain't no longer no eagle. A crow even less a crow. The water tower now as high as Rarden could go in the flat delta, and he went there all the time. He was drunk and he was there all the time, and if people had been afraid of him when he was flying, they were downright terrified of him now. He was gone, they'd say at the barbershop and at the hardware store and on the sidewalks, and say *I told you so, I told you,* and shake their heads. Everyone just waiting for part two to see what he would do. *I'll bet he'll go back North,* they'd say, and *I'll bet he'll blow his head off,* some would laugh, and some just, *Goddamn,* and maybe chuckle that De La Palma had Naomi back, which was, like I said, a thing no one knew for sure but knew too. Because even during the day you could see him up there, tiny as a dot at the top of that ladder, and his feets dangling over the side. His FELICITY JANE painted behind him in candy-apple red. And at night he slept there, and I would climb up hand over hand up that ladder and would sit and drink with him. He wouldn't say nothing, and I wouldn't say nothing back neither. Just sitting up there and swiping the Old Crow back and forth. The bridge you could see from there where we sat, but it wasn't nothing no more. It was just a bridge. No longer a test. *The* test of his art. Our craft. I had done it only three times, but those three times were the best three things I had ever done or have done, or I feel safe to say, will ever do in this life. There was still the swatches of land. But it wasn't the same. We were squirrels high up in a single tree where once we had been birds. So drunk I can't even say, so that I woke with the sun kicking my head, Rarden sitting on the edge, the empty bottle caught between his knees. I picked up my aching noggin and said, *Shit, man. Shit.* Shaking. And he turned and looked at me up and down like he didn't have no idea who I was and I had just got there anyhow.

But me imagining those nights, her with him, in the air again, her on his lap on a Saturday night with her pretty buckskin skirt hiked up to her waist, I can imagine, flying, her handling the stick, him the rudders, together like that, together, and the other way too, and taking the bridge, like that, right like that, fitted, heads back, yelling all they worth. Just sitting there and imagining that. Always imagining them like that. Still. Her. This kind of love. After everything.

Naomi went back to Nadine's and Nadine took her back because De La Palma asked her to, and I went back into the fields—stalled long as I could, drinking on the water tower and pleading we get out of that place, go someplace else, work up the stake for another Jenny—but then had to climb back down, put my feet on solid ground and hitch up into that tractor, snatching glimpses of the blue from under my cowshed, slow-crawling down them long rows. And that was the first time I ever saw Rarden angry—though I seen him drunk and shouting or into a silence plenty of times—when Naomi took back that job. He busted up our partner shack. Trashed it. Made kin'lin' of the chairs, hatched the table. Smashed the lantern, and then he set it all afire. We were just sitting there and drinking and talking nothing back and forth when he just stood up and swung down that first chair, and I said *Goddamn!* splinters going everywhere. But his eyes was wild with whiskey, and I don't think he even heard me. He grabbed up the lantern and crashed it to the floor. Me just sitting there in the almost dark and thinking *What the fuck?* and watching and not even really believing what was happening yet. Until he went for the ax

and buried it into the table, so that I had to jump back to
get missed and yelled, *God-damn-it, man! You crazy!* But he
wasn't listening. Rarden wasn't even there. I grabbed him
by the shoulders to stop him, and that's when he turned on
me, didn't say nothing, just rushed me backwards screaming into the wall. We hit and fell and then he had me against
the stove and his fists and teeths coming from every which
where so that it felt like there was a whole gang of him. And
me throwing one or two, but bigger and heavier and somehow coming out rolling up on top and punching him good
so that I couldn't stop until I stopped him and he was just
laying there gasping like a bellied fish and I got up off him
and his blood and mine too on my hands wiping my bloody
nose and left saying, *Goddamnit, Rarden. Just goddamnit
man*. And shaking my head.

And that was the same night she killed him. In self-defense,
the *Herald* said. Rape attempt was understood, because they
wrote it so you couldn't understand it in no other way. So
while that fire was eating our partner shack, me laying on
the cool dirt between two rows of waist-high cotton, thinking about what I had just done and touching my ribs and
licking at the gash of my knuckles and watching them
flames lick up that night, that fire breathing our shack all
the way down to the smoldering hell ground, he, Rarden,
had dragged himself up, busted lip and nose and blackening
eye that I imagine and all, thinking how I hit him and could-
n't stop hitting him, and was at Nadine's drinking. And I
hear that he called her a whore, and gnashing my teeth to
think to think of it, for *him*, Rarden, to say that about her—
hanging at the end of his own rope. People sitting in the
booths there heard that and the fact that he was at Nadine's
was in the *Herald*. And her working there and sure nobody
going to stop anyone from calling her a whore or anything

else for that matter. Him the only one, and it was him calling her that. I imagine that he even grabbed her between her slim thighs, treating her like what she was and what he had spent hisself proving she wasn't. This while the flames ate our shack and I lay hidden between the cotton, nursing my ribs, my busted jaw, the jags of light catching the crowd of people's mouth who had come out to watch in *ooohs* and *aaaahs*. Naomi working back at Nadine's, and me back on the spring seat of that tractor, up under that cowshed. And I can see Naomi's face too when he called her that, *whore*, bashed, imagine, coming from the only person she would've taken offense to it from, but him saying it, and her doing it all for him too, though she should've known he couldn't never see it that way, *whore*, so that in the end she had to take his hand from out under her skirt and lay down her apron on the counter and lead him like that out the door.

They were found naked, on the trestle, in the middle, where underneath there was the ancient turnstile to raise the sides. Rarden was naked and shot dead nine times. And I can't help but shudder at that quiet awful time she had taken to reload the revolver and start again—the six slow smacked shots and that silence as she emptied the chambers and reloaded shell by shell and started in again, pulling the trigger three more times, waiting for the slap of each bullet to ricochet away between the riverbanks before she shot him again. Found her naked, her feet dangling over the side, staring into the moon-wrinkled water which she had skimmed so wildly, carefully, screaming, on Rarden's lap, the pistol, one of De La Palma's, which it was said, he had given to her to protect herself when he had gotten her back her job at Nadine's, still caught in her two hands. There was also whiskey involved. And from there, I've since checked, you can see that water tower, even at night, with a good moon, bright.

Now, after fifty years, she sits on the front porch of her cabin under the trestle, and snaps beans. Her hair gray and long down her back. The children, my grandchildren—I have grandchildren now and a wife of forty-five years—think she's crazy, the Old Indian Lady they call her, a witch, and race by, as good as any graveyard. We never really talk. We have never talked about him since. I don't think we ever talked much even before, but then we didn't have to. There was the sky, the air, flying, joining us all three. People still talk about that crazy Yankee and his Jenny from Ohio. But we don't. There was a time when I was in the air. I could fly. I got farther than most people, white or black. But not any more. On the ground again, I am any nigger, any joe, bob, harry, frank. Any man. Any woman. Any slave. Slave to the small things I know and have never let myself escape. And even my own kids, my grandkids, don't believe I was once free. And my one witness, Naomi, who could tell them it was true, is grounded under that old trestle. And when I bounce by her on my tractor every morning or every evening on my way back to the shop, she looks up from her snapping beans and our eyes meet and we nod or I stop and ask her about her gardenias or say how humid it is out, but we don't talk about him. We never talk about him or that night, and I never want to. Me, I just want to remember him the way things was. The best thing I ever done. But maybe still asking myself as I swing the big 3640 into a day of cotton, *What is free?* It being maybe easier to say what's not free. That after fifty years.

Thanks

This book would not have been possible without the help of the following people. First, thanks to Phil Brady and Bob Mooney at Etruscan for believing in my work enough to publish it. Their vision for Etruscan as a small press that publishes high-quality literature is a noble one; I'm proud to be part of the endeavor. Thanks to Jane Wells, Richard Spilman, James Alan McPherson, Susan Dodd, Robley Wilson, Bob Shacochis, Ron Hansen, Doris Grumbach, and Larry Woiwode, who have influenced these stories. I would especially like to thank John Vernon and Barry Targan for their mentoring over the years. Thanks as well to the writers and editors who have supported the book: Andre Dubus III, Jayne Anne Phillips, Tom Perrotta, C. Michael Curtis, Joyce Carol Oates, Barry Targan, and Robert Coles. The quotation from Andre Dubus came to me on a postcard that he wrote some months before he died. I think of him every day. Thanks to Peter Herbert for his help pursuing the copyright permissions. Cathy Jewell, Managing Editor at Etruscan Press, did a fantastic job helping me prepare the manuscript to go to press. Her timeliness and professionalism have been a blessing. Gill Kent did a wonderful job copyediting. Elizabeth Woll's cover design is, I think, quite stunning, and it was a pleasure to work closely with her. The formidable editing skills of my wife, Sarah, were brought to bear on every page; my respect for her is present in every line.

SELINSGROVE
September 21, 2003

About the Author

Tom Bailey was born in Greenwood, Mississippi. Growing up he lived in North Carolina, Alabama, Florida, Virginia, and West Virginia. He is the author of *A Short Story Writer's Companion* (2001) and the editor of *On Writing Short Stories* (2000). Widely published in literary journals and magazines, including *DoubleTake*, his fiction has been reprinted in such anthologies as *The Pushcart Prizes* and *New Stories from the South* and cited in *The Best American Short Stories*. He is the recipient of a Newhouse Award from the John Gardner Foundation and was awarded a National Endowment for the Arts Fellowship in Fiction. Tom Bailey teaches at the Writers Institute at Susquehanna University in Selinsgrove, Pennsylvania, where he lives with his wife, Sarah, and their three children, Samuel, Isabel, and William. This is his first book of stories. Etruscan Press will publish his first novel, *The Grace That Keeps This World*, in fall 2004.